T.M. CROMER

COPYRIGHT

To Pamela R.
Your generosity of spirit knows no bounds.
Thank you for all you do.

THE THORNE WITCHES

THE THORNE FAMILY TREE

PRESTON THORNE

ALASTAIR THORNE — BOOK 6

TRINA GILLESPIE

PRESTON THORNE M **AURORA FENNELL**

RYKER GILLESPIE M **GIGI THORNE**

NASH THORNE — BOOK 7

HOLLY THORNE — BOOK 5

SUMMER THORNE — BOOK 1

AUTUMN THORNE — BOOK 2

WINTER THORNE — BOOK 3

SPRING THORNE — BOOK 4

The Thorne Witches

The Carlyle Family Tree

Carlyle

Tristan Carlyle — m — Glory Ashbrooke

Phillip Carlyle — m — Kiera Palmer

Robert Knox — Marianne Carlyle

Zane Carlyle
BOOK 3

Keaton Carlyle — m — Diane Marshall
BOOK 2

Cooper Carlyle
BOOK 1

Knox Carlyle
BOOK 4

Chloe Carlyle

CHAPTER 1

NINE YEARS AGO...

*T*oday was the day.

Today, she intended to confess her deepest, darkest secrets to Keaton. It was past time. After all these months together, he deserved to know the truth.

Stomach in knots, Autumn Thorne cut through the dense woods between their family estates. In the clearing between the two adjoining pieces of land, Keaton would be waiting.

"Keaton," she said with a sigh. Her forever love.

Family legend held that any born of the Thorne bloodline would only have one true soulmate. No other love would they take. It didn't matter, because Autumn had found hers, and she was more than content. She was blissful.

Ten months earlier, they both had returned to Leiper's Fork from their respective colleges. Full of dreams and high hopes for the future, she had uncharacteristically agreed when her best friend, Diane, suggested a casual graduation celebration at the local restaurant.

Keaton Carlyle had been seated at the long, glossy pine bar with two of his friends and his cousin. With his shaggy dark hair, eyes the shade of the aquamarine waters of the Caribbean, and a quick-to-flash sunny smile, he'd made many women's hearts flutter.

Autumn had been no exception. The moment she entered the overcrowded room, Cupid's arrow had lodged in her heart with a resounding thwack. From that very second on, she'd only had eyes for Keaton.

And he for her.

She laughed in remembrance of their initial meeting.

Both had been struck dumb in the presence of the other.

Wine flowed freely as they hid in the dark corner of the room and ignored everything and everyone. The magic of the alcohol had done its trick and eased them into a flirty conversation. Within twenty minutes, they'd set a time and location for their first date.

That night had been the beginning of a beautiful relationship. One that far exceeded anything Autumn could've dreamed. Keaton was an attentive lover who catered to her every whim, and she adored the very ground he walked on.

"True love," she murmured. Rare and precious.

Last night, he'd hinted at a future together, going so far as to ask what type of stone she wanted should he choose an engagement ring. The answer was obvious: aquamarine to match his incredible eyes.

When she at last reached the clearing, she found him half asleep on a blanket under the large oak tree. For a moment she stared, unable to catch her breath. He was beautiful in all the ways that mattered, and he was hers.

"Hey, babe," Keaton greeted with a lazy grin. He held out his arm, and she curled into him.

She rested her head on his chest and listened to his steady heartbeat.

"Keaton?"

"Mmm."

"Were you serious last night?"

"Mmhmm."

She lifted her head and met his sleepy gaze. "Why are you so tired?"

"Late night. One of the horses was colicky." He rolled on top of her and pinned her arms over her head with one of his hands. The other quickly found its way under her sundress and explored the waistband of her panties. He inched his fingers beneath the lace and touched her most sensitive area. "But not too tired to make love to you." He grinned and lowered his head to capture her lips.

Autumn broke their kiss before they became too heated. "Keaton, we need to talk."

He lifted his dark head to judge her earnestness. "Can't we talk *after*?"

"No. I need to tell you something."

"So serious!" he teased, flaring his eyes wide.

She smiled despite herself. His fun, laid-back attitude was easy to adopt.

"Will you promise me, whatever I tell you doesn't leave this clearing?"

"Of course." He sat up and pulled her to rest between his long legs.

"I've thought about how to say it a million times. I don't know how."

Keaton ran his index finger along her temple and tucked a stray lock of hair behind her ear. "Just stay it, babe. It can't be that dire." He grew still. "Unless you plan to break up with me. Is that what this is about?"

"No! Goodness, no. I love you, Keaton, and I want us to be together for always."

He sighed and hugged her tight. "For always."

Because there was no way to soften the words she needed to say, she blurted, "I'm a witch."

"Pardon?"

"I'm a witch."

He laughed.

A sick ball of dread formed low in her belly. *He thought she was kidding.*

"Keaton."

Her serious tone penetrated his amusement.

"Babe, there's no such thing as a witch."

She shifted to kneel in front of him. "There *is*."

"Is this like a Wiccan thing? Where you worship the trees and shit? I'm cool with that; just don't tell my mother. She might flip."

"No, it's not a Wiccan thing. They aren't witches in the real sense of the word."

"Autumn, come on. I'm too tired for game playing today."

A demonstration was in order. "Watch."

Autumn held her hand out flat and concentrated. She pulled from her element and created a beautiful, glowing fireball. The orange-red flame pulsed and danced in her hand. Smiling, she shifted her gaze to Keaton and froze.

His horror-filled eyes were locked on the flame.

Her earlier dread returned with a vengeance. "Keaton?"

"You're a witch," he croaked.

"Y-yes." She balled her fist and extinguished the fire. "I've wanted to tell you so many times. I—"

With his gaze still locked onto where the flaming ball had been, he asked, "Do you cast spells and things like that?"

"Yes. But only—"

"Love spells?" he demanded, expression hardening.

Her nervous laugh came out stilted and uneasy. "No. There's no such thing as a love spell."

"What about an obsession or desire spell?"

His angry intensity unnerved her. She had no idea where he was going with this.

"I suppose there are spells like that, but—"

Once again, he cut her off. "Remove it."

Autumn swallowed past her suddenly parched throat and wet her lips. "Pardon?"

"The spell you cast on me. I want you to remove it."

"Baby, I never put a spell on you."

He scrambled to his feet. "You're a liar!"

"No! I'm not lying. There's no spell."

"This explains so much," he ranted as he paced. "God, I'm stupid!"

She stood and tentatively approached him with her hands held out. "Keaton, it's me. I'm still the same person. I love you. And I promise, there is *no* spell."

Hands tucked behind his back, he skipped out of her reach as if her touch were contagious. "*Don't fucking touch me!*"

Shocked by his behavior, Autumn's own turmoil bubbled inside. His attitude had become completely unreasonable. "Why are you behaving like this?" she demanded.

"Because I don't like having my free will taken from me." He gripped his scalp and shook his head. "Christ, this explains so much," he repeated.

"What? What exactly does it explain?"

"My obsession with you. You're always on my mind. Even my dreams are filled with you." He pointed to her face, and his countenance hardened, growing ugly in his rage. "*You* did this to me. I don't know whether you thought it would be funny, or whether you honestly believed this is a way to tie a man to you, but the game is *over*, sweetheart." His tone was scathing and bitter at the same time.

Shock held her immobile. Speechless and hurt, all she could do was stare.

"If you won't remove the spell, I'll find someone who will. When I'm through with you, your name will be worthless in this town. No man will come near you."

Tears seeped from her eyes. She swiped at them in a vain attempt to hide her devastation. "Why are you being nasty? There's no spell."

"You want to play it that way? *Fine*. Don't say I didn't warn you."

"Keaton, you promised me you wouldn't say anything," she cried. "You promised."

"You remove the spell and stay the fuck away from me, and I'll *consider* keeping quiet."

Pressure built in Autumn's chest. *This must be what if felt like to have a heart attack.* The inability to take a deep breath, the sheer agony of the heart struggling to beat, the knowledge that the end of something precious was imminent.

The breeze picked up, and the trees around them began to sway. Back and forth they bent under the pressure of the howling wind. Branches cracked and plummeted to the earth with loud thuds. The blanket swirled up from the ground, caught against his legs, then whipped free to disappear on the air current.

Keaton lost his tan. "What the fuck?"

Lightning struck the ground on the opposite side of the clearing.

"If you're doing this, Autumn, knock it off!" he shouted over the building elements.

Words whispered through the tree and spoke to her. In her mind's eye, she pictured the athame from her altar. When it appeared in her hand, Keaton jerked in fear.

She didn't have time to cast a circle. He would bolt by then. Improvisation was required, and with the wickedly sharp tip, she scored her palm. "I bind thee, Keaton John Carlyle."

"What the fuck are you doing? *Autumn!*"

"I bind thee. Never shall you reveal the truth about me or any of the Thornes. Not in word, not in writing, not in gesture, not in deed. I bind thee from revealing the truth." She lifted her face to the sky and spread her arms wide, palms facing upward. "Goddess hear my plea. Grant me the power to bind this man's speech."

Lightning zipped sideways across the sky and struck the tree behind Keaton's back. His involuntary yell echoed around the clearing.

"You crazy bitch!" His words ended in a gurgle, and he clawed at his throat. Fear filled his bulging eyes, and his face turned an alarming shade of purple.

For a brief moment, Autumn's own throat seized in response. Young witches couldn't always control their power, and she worried her impromptu spell may have collapsed his larynx. When his face returned to a more normal shade, he cursed again.

She breathed a sigh of relief. While she might be angry with him, accidentally killing him would've left her devastated.

He stormed to where she stood in the center of the clearing. "What did you do to me?" he rasped.

"I neutralized your threat."

Wide-eyed, his gaze shifted to the bloody knife in her hand. "You stay away from me. Do you hear me?"

Keaton beat a hasty retreat and ran away as fast as his legs could carry him.

Energy depleted, Autumn stumbled to the flattened grass where their blanket had been. Kneeling, she ran her hand over the indentation their bodies had left. How had it gone so wrong so fast? How was it possible to feel such an aching hollowness inside, to feel on the brink of death, and yet continue to breathe?

She placed a hand on her lower abdomen. She'd never had a chance to tell him about the baby they'd made. Based on his reaction, another revelation was out of the question for the moment. With a silent prayer to the Goddess that her binding spell would remain solid, Autumn curled into a tight ball on the ground.

Grief caught up to her. Harsh, hiccuping sobs shook her frame, and all she could do was give herself over to the pain. Hours passed, and the sun set. Still she remained unable to drum up the energy or will to move.

She stared at the overhead stars peeping through the branches of the mighty oak. Oh, to be there! Far, far away from the hell she was experiencing here on Earth.

A beam of light settled on her face.

"Autumn?"

She turned her head toward her sister's voice.

Winnie rushed to her side. "Sister? What's wrong?" When she noticed the smattering of blood, she freaked. "Tums, where are you hurt? Where is the blood coming from?"

Autumn opened her mouth to speak. All but one word eluded her. "Keaton," she rasped.

"Is it Keaton? Did something happen to him?"

The tears she thought had dried up flowed once again. Warm, loving arms wrapped around her and pulled her close.

"Tums, talk to me. Was Keaton hurt?" Winnie asked urgently.

"No, but I can't talk about it. I just want to go home."

"Okay. Hold on."

With a quick incantation, Winnie teleported the two of them back to Thorne Manor.

"Why don't you go lie down. I'll bring you a sandwich and a cup of tea," Winnie suggested.

"Honestly, I don't think I can keep anything down right now." Autumn hugged her sister and drew in some of her warm, healing energy. "But I love you for offering."

As she trudged upstairs to her room, she wondered if she shouldn't try to speak to Keaton one more time. Surely, he must've calmed enough to see reason?

She called his cell phone but received no answer.

Tomorrow. Tomorrow she would visit him and tell him about the baby. They could decide where to go from there. If he still didn't want to be part of her life, she'd raise their child on her own.

She'd been wrong to blurt out her secret without feeling the waters first. But she could afford to allow Keaton time to adjust to the shock. He would see this was all a misunderstanding. Keaton was level-headed and calm in most situations, and Autumn had no doubt he'd see reason.

W HEN MORNING DAWNED AND BROUGHT WITH IT A GLORIOUS sunrise, Autumn stood on the front porch step and absorbed the sun's rays. The warmth fed her soul and restored her faith to full power.

With a cleansing breath, she borrowed a page from her younger sister's book of optimism and headed to the Carlyle estate.

As Autumn pulled into the drive, a strange foreboding took hold.

Diane's yellow VW Bug was parked outside the Carlyle house, and Autumn couldn't help wondering why her friend would be here this early. While Diane had made no secret of the fact she'd be happy to hook any of the Carlyle brothers or cousins, she hadn't had any luck in gaining their interest.

Keaton's brother, Cooper, answered her knock. "Hey, Coop. Is Keaton home?"

His handsome face took on an unhealthy shade of green.

"Coop?"

"He… uh, now's not a good time, Autumn."

Nausea churned in her stomach. As her unease grew, she worried she might lose the half muffin she'd managed to choke down this morning.

The truth was written on Coop's face. The pained sympathy. The distaste for what she was about to be put through.

Without another word, she shoved by Coop and raced for Keaton's room.

CHAPTER 2

PRESENT DAY

"*W*ord on the street is that you are the most skilled witch to train us," Keaton said by way of greeting.

If asked, Autumn would have said the only way Keaton would've given her the time of day was if she were the absolute last woman on earth, especially after their tumultuous history.

However, everything had changed a few weeks ago when Keaton learned he was a warlock whose powers had been bound at birth. Now that those powers were unbound, they radiated off him. To Autumn, he appeared brighter than the sun. And like peering at the sun, it hurt to look at him.

The irony of their little meeting today was not lost on her. A little over nine years ago, he'd shunned her because she was a witch. Now he sought her out because he needed her to teach him how to use his magical abilities.

Odd how, after all this time, his deep baritone still had the ability to reach right inside her and warm her lady parts. Because her body's reaction to him irritated her, she raised a brow and placed her hands on her hips. "We can start as soon as we get your apology out of the way."

He looked like he'd eaten sour grapes. His lips screwed up, and his eyes narrowed. "I'm sorry."

"For?" she asked tauntingly.

"Can we not leave the past in the past, Autumn?"

"Same old Keaton. Can't admit when he's wrong."

"Oh, and *binding me* from telling anyone you were a witch wasn't wrong? *Destroying* the project I worked on for so long with my daughter wasn't wrong?"

"I apologized for the truck and paid for the damages." Autumn shrugged as if she couldn't care less one way or the other when, in fact, she did. The damages she'd wrought to the restored truck back in the spring was bad form. At the time, she hadn't realized his daughter had had a hand in helping him rebuild his rust bucket. She believed she was only striking out at Keaton when she set the truck on fire.

"And?" he asked as tauntingly as she had a moment before.

"That's all you get. The binding spell was cast to protect myself and my sisters."

Anger caused red blotches high on his cheekbones and altered his normally tan complexion. It didn't detract from his male beauty. *And didn't that piss her right off?*

"You made me feel as if I was losing my mind. I couldn't talk about our relationship to anyone."

"We didn't have a relationship, Keaton. We were two stupid kids exploring sex. The term relationship indicates feelings, and you had none."

"That's not true," he argued, taking a step forward.

She held up a hand. "You know what? I've changed my mind. Keep your apology. I don't want to get into this." Down that path lay heartache, and she had no intention of trekking it again. She wished she'd never brought up the apology to begin with. "Go down and get Coop. We'll start the basics."

"Autumn." His tone had changed. It warmed enough to resemble the caring man she had thought she knew nearly ten years prior. In truth, that man never existed. *Not for her.*

"If you want me to teach you, we shelve the past, Keaton. No talking about it. *Ever.*" Because if she did, it would break the fragile walls she had in place around her heart. She needed those walls to elude the charming net he could so easily cast. Needed them to keep the pain and anguish of their breakup at bay.

The intensity in his deep-blue eyes disturbed her. Made her skin itchy and tight. He'd always seen too much. Her only saving grace was that those eyes weren't the loving ones she remembered. Time and pain had darkened his irises to a deeper, cloudier blue-green than they used to be.

Changing irises were a witch's or, in Keaton's case, a warlock's tell. The closest she'd gotten to him in recent years was a few months ago when he confronted her over setting fire to his truck. Because of her own hurt, she hadn't registered the change in color at the time. Had she done so, she'd have recognized him for what he was.

His daughter, Chloe, hadn't inherited his aquamarine eyes. Hers were a warm, golden shade of honey. It bothered Autumn to think that, eventually, some dickhead would come along and hurt little Chloe, too. Her eyes would lose that stunning color.

But such was life. Getting your heart bruised and battered was inevitable. She hadn't met an adult, certainly not a Thorne, who hadn't had a rough go of it.

"You're wasting my time, Keaton. You had two hours from when you showed today. Clock's ticking, buddy."

"I don't remember you as such a hard ass."

Autumn's inability to swallow came unexpectedly. She struggled through it. "Yeah, well, we all grow up." To create distance, she moved to the stand holding the Thorne grimoire and flipped through the pages. "It was bound to happen."

Because she could feel his gaze studying her profile, she tilted her head down and removed her hair clip. Her thick locks created a curtain, blocking his view.

"Thank you for being kind to Chloe." His husky voice came from close beside her and made her jump. Despite his six-foot-three, muscular frame, he moved as silently as a damned cat.

She inched sideways. To give herself something to occupy her hands, she touched a fingertip to the candle wicks around the room and lit each one in turn.

As far his daughter was concerned, Autumn could afford to be kind. "She's lovely, Keaton. A daughter anyone would be proud to call their own." *And she might have been theirs had things not taken such an ugly turn that day in the glen all those years before.* The thought had taunted her on more than one occasion. Whenever she saw the two of them together, laughing or sharing an ice cream in town, or whenever Chloe ran toward the Thorne gardens in search of Autumn's sister, Spring, the sight would stab Autumn right in the chest.

By now, Autumn was well practiced at shoving down her bitterness and anger. A few months ago, when she'd so carelessly set fire to the truck, she realized her destructive behavior had hurt an innocent. The wake-up call caused her to pack up, leave town, and re-evaluate her life.

"I worried about her reception here when C.C. first mentioned she... we were... like you."

He stumbled over his words and triggered her first genuine laugh.

"You make it sound like some dreaded disease you happened to catch." She sobered. "It's a gift from the Goddess. You should be proud to be from a powerful line. There aren't many pure-blooded witches or warlocks left. Most have been bred out of existence. And about your daughter..." She offered some semblance of a smile. "I don't hold the sins of the parents against the child."

"Bred?"

Apparently, he chose to ignore her dig about "the sins of the parents," and Autumn was happy to ignore the topic if he was.

She shrugged. "Throughout history, pure-bloods have married non-magical humans. Any children they created would've only received diluted abilities. Like Chloe." She finished lighting the candles and brushed her hands together. "Some witches bound their children to give them a normal life, or what they believed would be normal. Not unlike what your mother and father did to you, Coop, and your cousin, Zane."

Keaton frowned. "What about Knox? He's a Carlyle."

"I've only spoken ten words to Knox in as many years. I haven't had much interaction with your family and wouldn't know."

"I should ask him."

"I can't believe it hasn't come up in the weeks since you've found out the truth," she said as she stopped a few feet from him.

"He's been away, acquiring new breeding stock for our herd, and hasn't been around."

"Gotcha." No skin off her nose either way. She checked her watch. "We're down to one hour and forty-five minutes of training time left."

"You're going to be a stickler about this, aren't you?" he said softly.

"I am. I have a busy schedule, and I don't appreciate my time being wasted."

The hard edge crept back into her voice, but she'd be damned if she could prevent it. She didn't want to train Keaton. But a favor was a favor, and Autumn had grudgingly promised her sister, Summer, that she'd teach Coop and his brother. Since Summer's own powers were hit or miss most days, it fell to Autumn or one of their other sisters. And because those sisters had actual money-producing businesses, Autumn was the one chosen to help the newbie warlocks.

"Where did the carefree girl go? The one you used to be?" he mused aloud.

Tears burned behind her lids, and resentment gnawed at her insides. She presented her back and stared out the large attic window. From her vantage point, she could see the clearing where her life had gone to hell in a handbasket. "She was an idiot. And thankfully, no longer exists." *She died with her unborn fetus.*

"I miss her."

The wistfulness in his voice triggered her outrage. Where did he get off being sweet after all this time? Livid, she struggled to keep her voice level. "I don't. Like I said, she was an idiot." She consulted the time again. "One hour and forty minutes."

KEATON OBSERVED THE TENSION IN AUTUMN'S STANCE.

She hated everything about him occupying her space. It was in the defiant angle of her chin, her harsh dismissal of the past, and her eagerness to be done with teaching him and his brother the basics of witchcraft.

He hadn't wanted to learn and had initially rejected Coop's revelation last month—*especially* if it put him in close proximity to Autumn. But when his parents had returned and removed the binding, Keaton felt the supercharged energy pulse through his body on a cellular level. Finally, he understood.

Magic was like a powerful sword he needed to learn to wield for the safety of everyone around him. If he walked around untrained, he might unintentionally let loose one day and hurt someone.

His father and mother had expressed regret for their lie, and because of who they were, because he'd known them to be loving and generous parents, Keaton's only choice had been to forgive. In forgiving them, he'd been forced to compare their actions to Autumn's. If he was honest with himself, he had to acknowledge her magical crimes against him were much less life altering.

"You wanted an apology. I'm sorry, Autumn. Truly."

She jerked as if struck.

The urge to touch her overwhelmed him, but he curbed the impulse. He didn't have the right, not anymore. He had killed her love. Maybe not with his words in the clearing, but definitely when he'd slept with Diane the same night of their breakup. He'd never had the opportunity to make it right before he found out Diane was pregnant with his child.

"Look, if your intent is to stand around jawing, then I need to get to my real work." She headed for the door without sparing him a glance. "I'll catch you later."

Before she could leave, Coop stepped into the room.

"You're late," she snapped as she shoved a lock of auburn hair behind her ear.

Coop flashed her the patented Carlyle grin. One glimpse of those pearly whites was guaranteed to set fire to the panties of unsuspecting females everywhere.

Keaton had a moment of unease when he saw the twin spots of pink bloom on Autumn's cheeks. *Was she attracted to his brother?*

He released his pent-up breath when Autumn said, "Your charm doesn't work on me, Sheriff. Save it for Summer. Tomorrow, if you aren't on time, you can find another sucker to teach you. I have better things to do than wait around for you while you flirt with my sister."

"You're warming up to me, Autumn. I can tell," Coop teased as he tapped a fingertip to her nose.

Keaton called on every ounce of self-control not to rip his brother's arm off for touching her. He didn't want to *think* what it meant that he was still territorial after all these years.

Autumn snorted. "Pfft. Keep dreaming, Coop." To Keaton, she asked, "Do you want Chloe to join us for future classes? I know she's learned a few things from Spring, but she's more than welcome to come with you tomorrow."

Her generosity surprised him and shook him out of his pique. What kind of woman would offer to help the daughter of the woman you screwed in a drunken stupor? "I'll ask her tonight."

"Great. Now, let's get started." She tapped the book on the altar. "This is a spell book, also known as a grimoire. Every magical family has one. It is handed down through each generation. These books can be hundreds or, depending on the family, thousands of years old. Your family should have one, too." She ran a hand lovingly over the binding. "Most spells are in Latin, although there are a few in our grimoire in another language that we've been unable to identify. I'm sure your family's book is the same."

"I thought a lot of people didn't know how to write in the old days," Keaton said as he inched closer to get a look at the book she held.

"The book is like a magical version of Dragon Dictation. You can speak a spell, and it will appear on the pages."

"Dude! That's badass." Coop reached for the grimoire. "May I see it?"

"No." She softened her sharp answer with a half-smile. "Not yet, anyway. I'll explain why later."

Keaton studied her as Autumn droned on about the altar and the best wood for magical purposes when creating one. She hadn't changed much. Her ivory skin was still as flawless. The deep auburn hair still caught the light and glowed red in its beam. Her lips were just as full, and her body... *God, her body.* At thirty-two, the woman had the same tight, toned body she'd had as a twenty-two-year-old.

His skin tingled in remembrance of holding that curvy body against his own. Of tasting every inch. Of being cradled between those long legs. He mentally shook himself. If he didn't stop, he'd be sitting here with serious wood popping up—and not the magical altar type.

With a suspicious glance in his direction, she went on to explain the process of casting a circle. Apparently, magic was to be done within this circle for a number of reasons. The most important was to protect the spell caster. She also explained the purification steps before a ceremony.

While Autumn answered his brother's questions, Keaton put his finger on what bothered him about her appearance. Her eyes. Once a bright, beautiful shade of light amber, they were now an average murky brown. How was that possible? It was as if all light had escaped them.

"When can we get to the good part?" Coop asked and rubbed his hands together.

"Slow your roll, Sheriff. Until you learn the rules, you don't perform magic."

"Rules?" Keaton asked, drawn back into the conversation.

"Rules," she said. "Number one, do as you will, and it harm none. In other words, magic is never to hurt or strike out at another."

Keaton's brows shot up, and he snorted. "I'd say you broke that rule."

Autumn turned incredulous eyes on him. "Are you serious right now?"

"I'm just saying, when you—"

Coop clapped a hand over Keaton's mouth and wrestled him to the floor. "Shut up, you idjit! She already hates you. Do you want her to shish kebab you?"

"Are you two done? We are down to only an hour left," she informed them. The cold tone left little doubt how much she despised Keaton's presence in her home.

"Number two, you don't use magic for personal gain." She stared directly at Keaton. "No spells or binding potions for love, revenge, or financial gain. Nothing that doesn't benefit the whole. Remember, do as you will, and it harm none."

She knelt and gestured for him and Coop to do the same. "There are other rules, but those are the most important. I'll be sure to have a list of the others for you tomorrow morning. Now let's practice meditation. It's important to be centered before starting any spell."

With the breathing techniques she demonstrated, Keaton got a good grasp on how to calm and center his inner self. These would also be useful tools for his everyday life as the small town mayor where stress and mayhem were the name of the game.

Autumn went on to discuss ways to draw out their magic, the importance of discovering their individual elements, and the need to obtain a familiar to boost their spell-casting power. "You are to try nothing on your own. Is that clear? *Nothing.* Not even the smallest spell. I will tell you when you are ready. All spells should be cast in a dedicated circle. That is tomorrow's lesson. I'll see you at eight a.m. sharp. Don't be late, or we're done."

CHAPTER 3

"*I* think she's softening toward me," Keaton said, taking a bite of his breakfast sandwich and following it up with a sip of coffee. The *she* didn't need to be clarified. Only one woman of his acquaintance hated him, and they both knew who that woman was. *Autumn Thorne.*

The wry look Coop sent him said it all.

"What? You don't think so?"

"Dude, you are so delusional it isn't funny." Coop took a sip of his own black coffee. "She tolerates you as a favor to Summer. I suspect if you were on fire, she wouldn't work up the spit to try to put the flames out."

His brother was correct. Still, she hadn't teleported Keaton to hell, so that went in the plus column. "She's sweet with Chloe though."

"That surprises you?"

"Yeah, considering Chloe was the result of my affair with another woman."

Coop stopped his visual study of the diner's occupants—when on sheriff duty, he stayed alert—and pinned Keaton with a stare. "You didn't have an affair. You impregnated and married another woman."

Heat crept up Keaton's neck. "Except for the result of my daughter, it was the biggest mistake of my life."

His brother snorted and took another sip of coffee. The "ya think?" was implied.

"Do you believe it's possible to miss the love you thought you had after all this time?" Keaton asked.

"I guess. I mean, if Summer had never come back after I drove her away, I probably would've gone to my grave regretting that I'd screwed things up between us."

Rarely did the two of them talk about their innermost feelings. It felt odd to do it now, but Keaton finally had the ability to articulate what he felt after nearly ten years of silence. Thanks to Coop, Autumn's spell had been broken. Albeit accidentally, but Keaton was grateful to his brother all the same.

"Do you still love her?" Coop asked quietly.

"I don't know. Probably not. But being around her these past few days has brought back a lot of the memories I'd locked away." Keaton traced the pattern on the Formica tabletop. "My anger had kept me going all this time."

"You're not angry anymore?"

"I am—to an extent. But I'm beginning to understand she had a lot to lose. Why she didn't trust me to keep quiet, I'll never understand."

"You reacted badly, Keaton. She told you what she was, and you freaked the fuck out on her. What was she supposed to think?"

"I know." Keaton shoved his half-eaten breakfast away, appetite gone. "She won't let me explain. It's driving me nuts."

Over the last week, Autumn had maintained a strictly professional attitude. Whenever he had arrived early or tried to stay a little late after their lesson, she would paste on a false smile and come up with some excuse to cut the conversation short.

"It's not like I can show up later in the day and force her to see me. She goes back to her home in Maine directly after our sessions are over," Keaton complained.

"As soon as you learn to teleport, you can follow her."

"Right." A comfortable silence fell between the brothers as they sipped their coffee.

"I still dream of her," he confessed.

Coop paused with the mug halfway to his mouth. "Autumn?"

Keaton nodded. "Nearly every night. I've never stopped. Not really."

The shocked expression on Coop's face nearly made Keaton laugh.

"Nine years is a long time. Maybe you should talk to a therapist," Coop suggested, not unkindly.

"You don't think it's normal?"

"No, I don't. *Especially* not almost every night. That seems like an unhealthy obsession."

"Yeah. Maybe you're right. I—"

The woman in question sailed through the door.

Keaton's breath halted in his chest.

She was stunning. With her dancing eyes and a simple flick of her auburn hair, Autumn challenged the world at every turn. Added to her sparkling wit was a tall, magnificent body with the kind of curves to make grown men beg. And she held the power to make his palms itch with the desire to touch her.

Yes, he definitely still held an unhealthy obsession for her.

As he watched, she flirted with Old Man Harkins from the hardware store. She caught the old pervert's hand before it reached her ass. With a wave of one finger and a kiss on his weathered cheek, she set Harkins straight. The old curmudgeon actually blushed.

Keaton couldn't blame the guy. Autumn had that effect on men—young and elderly alike. She'd certainly had the same effect on *him*. Perhaps that was why he had believed she'd bewitched him in the literal sense of the word. He'd been unable to think of anything but her. Whatever Autumn wanted, he would've killed to provide for her. Thank God—er, the Goddess—that she never knew the power she possessed back then. Because if she had, she'd have owned the world by now.

Their eyes connected in the mirror behind the counter. Her teasing air disappeared, and she averted her gaze.

That had been her reaction over the last nine and a half years. It was as if it hurt her to look at him. He knew because it hurt him to look at her. Or maybe she only viewed him with disgust, and he was projecting his feelings on her.

"Daddy!"

Keaton's attention was torn away from Autumn at the sound of his daughter's exuberant voice. He rose and lifted her into his arms as she reached their table. "Hey, midget! Ugh, you're getting heavy. I swear you've grown an inch since I saw you last," he teased.

Father and daughter stared at one another, matching grins took up half their face.

Their moment was shattered by the arrival of Diane. "Do you want to tell him what you did, or shall I?" Her scowl telegraphed her displeasure.

Keaton wasn't surprised. His ex-wife was always pissed about one thing or another. Mostly at him, but her anger always seemed to be directed at poor Chloe of late.

"I got into mother's makeup," Chloe whispered tearfully.

"That doesn't sound so bad," Keaton said, giving his daughter an extra-tight squeeze then setting her on her feet on the booth seat.

"Do you know how much that makeup kit cost, Keaton?" Diane's voice climbed to shrill, and heads turned in their direction—Autumn's included.

Keaton tugged at his already open collar. Why did it feel like a noose was tightening around his neck every damned time he spoke to Diane?

He exhaled loudly. "Just let me know how much it costs, Diane. I'll see it is replaced."

"You should be grateful you have a daughter who wants to share in girly things with you," an arctic voice inserted.

Keaton's gaze shifted to Autumn, and he gave a subtle shake of his head.

"Well, if it isn't the homewrecker," Diane jeered.

His eyes closed, and he counted to ten. Same tune, different day. Diane had never gotten over her jealousy of Autumn.

Autumn's amused laughter snapped his eyes open. "Home-wrecker? That would imply I had an affair with your ex-husband while you were married, Diane." Autumn sidled up to Keaton and ran a hand up his chest. The Devil danced in her eyes.

This wasn't going to be good.

She hooked a hand around his neck and drew his head down to hers.

Or maybe it was.

When their lips connected, he heard gasps echo throughout the restaurant. *Oh, the curse of small-town living.*

He didn't care. The warm softness of Autumn's mouth on his was heaven once more. He became lost in the kiss, his tongue tangoing with hers. The dance, erotic and full of passion. He hadn't been aware of his right arm encircling her waist or of his left hand burrowing into her thick hair to keep her close until she drew back. He mourned the loss.

"Keaton and I never carried on while you were married. He's too honorable for that," Autumn directed to Diane while her eyes remained fixed on him. She sent him a saucy wink and faced his ex. "But now..." She gave a delicate shrug. "Anyway, like I said, you should be grateful for such an amazing daughter who wants to spend time with you. Those moments are gone before you know it."

Without a by-your-leave, she sashayed across the room, scooped up her bag of food from the counter, and breezed out the door in the exact carefree manner in which she arrived.

Seconds ticked by before anyone stirred or removed their focus from the closed door. As one, the patrons turned their gazes back to him.

He grinned, unable to help himself. He'd say one thing for the woman; Autumn sure knew how to make an exit.

AUTUMN CLIMBED BEHIND THE WHEEL OF HER JEEP AND RESTED HER shaking hands on the steering wheel. *What the hell had she done?* She kissed Keaton! Without thought to consequences, she'd jerked his head down to hers and laid one on him. Right there for all of Podunkville to see.

Their mutual passion hadn't died. It was oh-so-much better than she remembered. So good, in fact, that it would make for an awkward morning when he showed for training today and would probably give her a great many sleepless nights, too.

With a grimace, Autumn started the engine. She'd stirred up a hornet's nest. If she had a brain in her head, she'd park the jeep at her family's estate and pop back home to Maine, never to return.

But the kiss had been worth it to shut up that twat-waffle, Diane. The sanctimonious bitch had it coming. Oh, she preached a good game and made sure to appear every Sunday as the upstanding Christian, decorating the first pew with her prayer book in hand. Yet secretly, Diane was boinking the married pastor in his private office on Sunday afternoons while the guy's poor, unsuspecting wife fed the homeless at a Nashville mission.

Autumn prayed to the Goddess that the pastor's wife would catch those two in the act. She'd even thought about helping the discovery along with a little magic. Ultimately, she'd decided against it. Things had a way of working out. That skank would get hers.

Not for the first time, Autumn wondered if Diane had ever truly been her friend. In school, the two girls had been besties. Autumn had never suspected the deep jealousy and ill-will Diane had harbored toward her. The morning after Keaton had broken her heart, Autumn finally understood just how much. The triumph was as plain as day on Diane's face when Autumn had walked into Keaton's room and found the two of them in bed together.

She lost two people that day: Keaton and Diane. But then, she wondered if she'd ever truly had either of them, if they ever truly cared about her. Perhaps that was why she found it difficult to befriend anyone now.

Oddly enough, her misplaced affection for them was what made her kind to Chloe. In Keaton and Diane's child, she saw the ghost of Autumn's young, innocent self. A girl who wanted love and friendship.

Time would change the child. It would make her cynical and hard, but Autumn didn't need to be mean and contribute to the eventual realization that the world was a shithole filled with people ready to stab you in the back. No, she would help preserve innocence at every opportunity.

As she pulled into the driveway of Thorne Manor, she noticed Summer in a heated discussion with Alastair. A grimace of distaste tugged at the corners of her mouth before Autumn could school her features.

He barely spared her a glance, but she sensed he missed nothing.

"Uncle Alastair," she drawled with false cheer as she exited her jeep. "To what do we owe this unwelcome visit."

Tension lined his shoulders and compressed his mouth into a thin line. "Your mother doesn't have much longer. I need the Chintamani Stone recovered."

Emotion clawed the back of her throat and made it difficult to swallow.

Mother.

Over the last few weeks, Autumn had tried not to think of her mom wasting away in stasis. Because when she did, rage—along with a major sense of betrayal—rocked her.

Her mother, Aurora, hadn't died twenty years ago like they were all led to believe. She'd taken off with Alastair Thorne to raise a secret child—Summer's twin. Five years later, some mysterious event took place that injured Aurora Fennell-Thorne and left her in a supernatural coma, neither living nor dead.

All this time wasted, and all the lies told. Autumn shook her head in disgust.

"I told you, when we get a better handle on its location, we'll retrieve it," Summer said. "Until then, I'm not going to the farthest reaches of the world on a wild goose chase just to please you, Alastair."

"You stubborn little fool!" he snapped. "This is your mother's *life* we are talking about."

"You aren't gaining brownie points by being an asshole, Uncle," Autumn warned, joining hands with Summer in a show of unity.

Frustration was written all over his countenance. "How do I get through to you? She's fading. If we don't act soon, she'll be lost to us forever."

The "us" stuck in Autumn's gullet. She didn't want her mother to wake only to abandon them for Alastair again. The thought was petty, but there, taking up space in her head and heart, nonetheless.

Summer, the softer and more compassionate of the two of them, dropped Autumn's hand and reached for Alastair's. "I'm working on it, Father. You have to trust that I'm doing my best."

Blue eyes, darker but identical in shape to Summer's, studied his daughter for a long moment. Finally, he nodded and squeezed Summer's hand, then he faced Autumn. "I'll give you a piece of advice, niece. Don't get in my way on this. Any affection I hold for your mother or sister won't soften my punishment should you double-cross me."

Autumn scoffed. "What could you possibly do to me?"

Coop's cruiser pulled into the drive and caught the attention of the three Thornes.

Keaton, Coop, and Chloe had arrived for the morning training session. Alastair watched them exit the vehicle before he turned back to her. His slow smile, laced with an edge of menace, made her stomach flip over. In an effort to appear unaffected, she slipped her standard icy mask in place.

"I think there is quite a lot I could do to you, my dear girl. You like to believe you are tough. Yet I wonder, should something happen to the man you love, something that you might have prevented, would you remain so sure of yourself?"

She lunged.

But Alastair was quick to throw up an invisible barrier between them.

Crashing into it wasn't at all fun, but she did no more than grunt.

"I'll see you in hell before I let you hurt an innocent, Alastair. You see if I don't," she promised.

"I want that stone," he said ominously.

In the blink of an eye, he was gone, leaving two very shaken sisters in his wake.

Across the distance, she met Keaton's concerned gaze. Uncaring mask firmly back in place, she pivoted on her heel and headed into the house.

CHAPTER 4

"*W*hat was that about?"

Because she suspected he'd follow her, Autumn wasn't surprised by Keaton's immediate appearance in the kitchen.

"Nothing you need concern yourself with," she said coldly as she tossed the bag of food on the counter and reached for a plate.

"Autumn, look at me."

She stopped, set the plate on the counter, and faced him.

"What's going on? Who is that man, and why did you go after him?"

"*That* was my dear Uncle Alastair. He's come up with a magical item for Summer to retrieve, and he's irritated she hasn't complied with his demands as of yet."

"Why does he want it?"

"Why, to bring my mother back to life," she said with mock cheerfulness. "I'm surprised Coop hasn't informed you of all this by now."

"He didn't." Keaton came farther into the room and stopped a foot from her. "After all this time? Your *mother*? Is bringing someone back to life actually possible?"

She released a weary sigh and looked out over the yard. "I don't know. But it might be possible for someone in stasis like my mom."

His large, warm palm settled on her lower back.

She told herself she shouldn't find comfort in the touch, that she was a fool to open up that particular can of worms. But his touch had always had a power all its own.

"What is stasis?"

"When someone is in the state between life and death, similar to a coma, but without the feeding tubes or respirators to sustain them. They are in a sleeping state but can't wake or die."

"Jesus! What do the doctors say?"

"Witch doctors you mean?"

His eyes widened, and she laughed in genuine amusement. He obviously didn't find her as funny as she found herself.

Autumn took pity on him and said, "Mother isn't in any hospital, Keaton. She's at Alastair's mansion in North Carolina. Summer's actually been to see her so we know he's not lying about *that* at least."

"How? I thought your mother died like twenty years ago or more."

"We did, too." She gave her standard shrug and went back to compiling a plate of the best biscuits and gravy Tennessee had to offer. "Apparently, we were misinformed."

"You didn't answer my original question. Why did you go after him?"

"Leave it alone, Keaton. It's really none of your business."

He took the plate of food from in front of her and held it aloft. "Somehow, I got the impression it was. Start talking."

"You *do* realize I can snap my fingers and have my plate back, right?" she asked dryly.

"You take all the fun out of being taller than you," he said and handed her the dish. "What he said, did it have something to do with me and Chloe?"

She stared, mesmerized by his intense gaze. Once upon a time, she would've thought the concerned expression was for her, now she knew it was only for himself and his daughter. Keaton had an innate sense of self-preservation, and on a subconscious level, he recognized Alastair's power.

"Yes. He likes to throw threats around, believing we will all fall in line. If I can help it, I won't let him hurt her."

Keaton stilled. "He'd hurt a child?"

"I don't think, when it boils down to it, he would. But I can't be certain." Autumn set her plate on the table and crossed to the silverware drawer. She busied herself with selecting utensils. "I lost my ability to read people a long time ago."

"Because of me." The grimness in his voice was unmistakable.

"Maybe, but only in part. I was too trusting back then." She sighed and poured herself a cup of tea then added a spoonful of sugar. "None of it matters and life goes on. Now, if you don't mind, I'd like to eat my breakfast before it congeals into a disgusting blob."

He nodded to the full pot of coffee in the brewer. "Do you mind?"

"If you must."

"Wow. I'd think you'd be a little nicer to me after exploring my tonsils less than a half hour ago. I feel so used and cheap."

She snorted the tea up and out her nose.

Without missing a beat, he tossed her the dish towel. "You okay, babe?"

Her glare said it all—as did his grin.

"If you keep it up, I'll let Alastair follow through on his threat to off you," she snapped. She froze when she realized her mistake. *Crap!*

His eyes went wide then sharpened on her flushed face. "He didn't threaten Chloe."

In an attempt to appear casual, she dumped sugar into her tea and stirred. When she took a sip, she gagged. *How much damned sugar had she added?*

"Four *tablespoons*," he said with a smirk. "Someone a little distracted?"

"Piss off." She rose and dumped the tea in the sink, disconcerted he'd read her mind. When Autumn turned around, Keaton blocked her path.

"Okay, just so I have this straight. Dear old Uncle Alastair threatened my life—*not* Chloe's—to manipulate you, and you were going to rip his head from his shoulders had he not thrown up some invisible force field when he did. Is that about right?"

She crossed her arms under her breasts and refused to answer.

"Why would his threat upset you unless you still care?"

"Perhaps it has nothing to do with *you* and everything to do with *me* not wanting to be manipulated. Did you ever think of that?"

Keaton shifted closer and invaded her space.

Autumn took a step back and held up her hands. "Back off, Keaton. I don't like being crowded."

"I'm not crowding you. I'm kissing you," he murmured against her mouth.

Whatever resistance she might've imagined she possessed melted the second she breathed in his unique scent. She was mush in the face of his sexual onslaught.

"Aww, hell," she muttered and threaded her hands through his thick dark hair to tug him closer.

Their second kiss was better than the first. The taste of coffee was on his tongue along with the hint of something sweeter. Keaton took his time, delving in again and again, teasing her response. The gentle love bite to her lower lip had her growling and raising a leg to hook around his hip. Her arms came around his head to hold him closer.

Before she knew it, his hands were under her shirt, tracing her ribs and inching her bra up over her breasts. When his thumb brushed her pebbled nipple, she moaned into his mouth.

In an about-face, Keaton jerked away and made haste to straighten her clothes. As she stood in confusion, he raked his hands through his hair to restore some semblance of order. Just in time, it seemed, because Chloe raced into the room and demanded her father's attention. "Daddy!"

Back against the counter, Autumn gripped the granite top with both hands, horrified by what she'd allowed to happen. She was shaken to her core. One low, sexy "I'm kissing you" and she turned into marshmallow fluff. So much for her mental and emotional walls. He'd taken a wrecking ball to those fragile blocks. If asked later, she wouldn't be able to say if she'd have allowed him to make love to her, but at the time, she sure wasn't applying the brakes to that out-of-control train.

The conversation swirled around her, and Keaton cast her the occasional side glance. His slight frown encouraged her to move, to say something—*anything*—but she couldn't.

Nine years of heartache—*nine damned years!*—and she'd caved with two kisses.

Furious with herself, with Keaton, and with the whole damned world in general, she shoved away from the counter and made tracks to her old bedroom. As she crossed the threshold, she halted.

Except for the sheet-less bed and a single box in the corner, the room was bare. Nothing about the space revealed the person who had lived there for nearly thirty-two years. But this wasn't her home anymore.

FROM THE CORNER OF HIS EYE, KEATON WATCHED AUTUMN FLEE THE kitchen.

She was upset. That much was obvious. Only he didn't know if it was because he'd guessed she reacted to protect him, their impromptu kiss, or because her uncle was putting demands on her. Perhaps a combination of all three.

"Daddy?"

He gave Chloe his undivided attention.

"Is Miss Autumn a homewrecker?"

Irritation gripped him, and he worked to dispel it. Chloe was only repeating her mother's words from earlier.

"No, midget, she's not. The true definition of a homewrecker is someone who breaks up, or attempts to break up, a happy family unit." He lifted his daughter onto a stool and poured her a glass of water as he formed the words to explain. "Chloe, I am never going to lie to you. There may be times I don't tell you everything you want to know, but it will be because the timing is wrong, not because you don't deserve to know. Do you understand?"

"Is now one of those times?"

Her inquisitive honey eyes peered up at him as she sipped her water.

"I married your mother because you were in her belly. We weren't in love. Not like your grandparents or Uncle Coop and Miss Summer. But I wanted to be your dad very much, and I thought marriage was the best option."

Her rapt attention caused an internal cringe. His explanation wasn't going to be cut and dried.

"But sometimes grown-ups don't always get along. That's what happened between me and your mom. We weren't a happy family unit. The only people who broke up our unit was me and your mom. Miss Autumn had nothing to do with that." *Liar, liar, pants on fire.* Autumn had been the ghost between them for their entire relationship.

"Good. I don't want her to be a homewrecker."

"Somehow, I doubt she ever will be. She's not the type." He ruffled her dark hair. "Why don't you finish your water? I need to go speak to Miss Autumn for a few minutes, okay?"

"Are you going to kiss her again?"

His jaw dropped. "Uh…"

"Like at the restaurant?"

"Oh, uh…" What could he say? Hell, yes, he would kiss her if given the opportunity. *More than that even.* He regained command of his tongue. "Finish your water."

She grinned into her glass, and he got the distinct impression the little troublemaker was playing him.

Keaton jogged up the stairs to Autumn's old room. Memories of hanging out, listening to music, and making love all flooded back. They'd been happy once. How something so beautiful could go wrong and turn into such ugliness was beyond his comprehension.

He found her sitting on the bed and staring at a brown cardboard box in the corner. The room was empty but for the mattress, bed frame, and box.

"It seems odd to see the room bare," he said softly as he leaned his shoulder against the jamb. "It used to be colorful. Awards, posters, pictures of us."

She remained silent and continued to stare at the box.

Keaton shoved off the door frame and entered her room. "Your vanity used to be here, didn't it?" He gestured to the wall closest to him. "I used to love to watch you play with your hair and try on new makeup." Remembered emotions clogged his throat. "You were the most beautiful thing I'd ever seen. Still are."

Her head came up, but she didn't look his way.

Abruptly, she stood.

He held his breath and waited for her to speak.

"The box is yours. I never could quite bring myself to drop it by your place since that day." She gave her standard careless shrug. "I guess I could've had one of my sisters drop it off, but I forgot. Anyway, be sure you take it when you leave today. I think Spring wants to make this a guest room."

She brushed by him and exited the room.

His eyes went to the box. On wooden legs, he retrieved it and set it on the bed. Without looking, he knew what he would find: every gift he'd ever given her. An MP3 player containing their favorite songs. Most likely every picture they'd ever taken together. Their entire relationship boxed up so she didn't have to look at it.

He closed his eyes and remembered the way they had been in those last few minutes before she told him the truth of what she was. Teasing, happy, in love. Not one second of one day spent with her had faded from his memory. Each moment was preserved in his mind. Etched in the very fabric of his existence. Periodically, he would take out those old memories and dust them off, remember what true happiness had felt like. But in the next breath, he'd get angry because he believed it had all been a lie. A spell she'd cast on him to entice him. He'd been such a stupid boy. Undeserving of her. Of them.

"Daddy?"

He glanced up.

"What are you doing?"

"Taking a stroll down memory lane."

"Oh."

He smiled because she had no idea what he meant, but she liked to pretend she did.

"Miss Autumn said to tell you to 'shake a leg, time's a-wastin'.'"

"She did, huh?" He forced a laugh. "Well, we mustn't keep Miss Autumn waiting."

CHAPTER 5

*T*hroughout witchcraft training 101, Autumn felt Keaton's hawk-like stare. It took all her willpower not to squirm under his constant regard. Mostly, she directed her lesson to Chloe and Coop. She only spoke to Keaton when he asked her a specific question.

She had each of them practice drawing from their element for a simple trick to test their ability. For Chloe, the test was to use air to extinguish only the candles along the back wall. The child manipulated the air as if she'd been born doing it.

"Great job, Chloe." Next, she gestured to Coop. "Fire if I'm not mistaken. You get to re-light the candles she put out."

When he looked uncertain, she took his hand in hers and extended his index finger. "Feel the pulse? It matches the beat of your heart. What you need to do is concentrate that energy into the tip of your finger. Visualize it all flowing in one direction. Don't shove the power; let it build slowly." She released him to step back. "Once you've harnessed the feeling, touch your finger to the wick."

After two failed attempts, Coop grasped the concept. His third try met with success.

"Brilliant!" She smiled and patted him on his upper arm. "Summer is going to be proud of your progress."

"I assume I'm done for the morning? I'll go tell her," he said and hurried away with a grin.

She had no doubt as to why he was truly going to find her sister. The two of them went at it like rabbits. Autumn tried to tamp down on her wistfulness since she hadn't had a lover in what felt like a millennium.

Chloe tugged her hand. "What's Daddy going to do, Miss Autumn?"

"If I'm not mistaken, your dad is a water element. Would you be kind enough to take that bowl over there and get some water from the bathroom down the hall?"

The girl, eager to complete her assigned task, grabbed the designated bowl and ran off.

Autumn couldn't help but smile again. With her dark bouncing curls and gap-tooth grin, the child was engaging.

"You're good with children. I'm surprised you haven't married and had a few of your own."

She dragged her eyes from the empty doorway to Keaton. "I'm not wife and mother material."

"Bull. You'd make a wonderful wife and an even better mother."

His husky statement was a knife to her heart. Once upon a time, she wished he'd said that exact thing to her. Wished he'd pulled her to him instead of pushed her away in his fear. She released an impatient breath. Dwelling on the past wouldn't gain her a thing.

"Can we keep things on a professional level, Keaton? I really don't wish to discuss my personal life with *you* of all people."

All expression was wiped clean, and his lids lowered enough to hide any feelings that might be reflected in his eyes. "Sure."

"Thanks."

Chloe chose that moment to return, careful to take small steps to prevent sloshing the water.

"Perfect," Autumn smiled again. If it appeared a little less sincere, she hoped the girl wouldn't pick up on it. To Keaton, she said, "It's the same concept I explained to Coop. Harness the pulse to one slow, steady stream."

"You aren't going to hold my hand like you did his?"

"You're a big boy. I'm sure you don't need anyone to hold your hand."

"But what if I want you to hold my hand?"

Now he was just messing with her. "Fine. We can hold hands." She spit in her hand and held it out.

Surprise, then laughter, lit his face. He gripped her hand and winked. "I'm not afraid of your saliva, babe." He leaned in to whisper, "I've sampled it many times."

She shoved his face away. "Stuff it."

With his voiced pitched only for her ears, he said, "Oh, now we're talking. I'd *so* love to stuff it."

Her cheeks felt hot, and she attempted to retrieve her hand from his grasp.

"Nope. You are holding my hand for this one." He kissed her knuckles. "What's the plan with the water?"

"Dumping it over your head would be my first choice," she muttered.

"I like this snarky side of you. My sweet Autumn has grown teeth," he teased.

This time she did jerk her hand away. "I'm not your anything. Not then. Not now. Not ever."

Her frosty tone left no one in doubt as to her seriousness.

She wiped her palm on her jeans. More calmly she said, "I want you to create a fountain of the water. Try to raise the center an inch or two above the rim of the bowl."

The water bubbled once and flattened out.

"You're not trying, Keaton. Concentrate."

Again, the water bubbled up.

With an impatient sigh, she grabbed his hand and felt for his power. "Again."

When the water only bubbled the third time, his problem became obvious. He was purposely stalling.

"Chloe? I need a private minute alone with your dad. Do you mind hanging out in the kitchen for a few minutes?"

"Okay."

"Awesome. If you're hungry, you can knock on Winnie's door and tell her I said to make you some of her delicious cinnamon rolls. How about that?"

The girl beamed and rushed forward to hug Autumn's waist. "I don't think you're a homewrecker, Miss Autumn. I wish *you* were my mom."

Autumn's heart lurched. Had she not miscarried, her child would be the same age as Chloe. There were moments, like these with Keaton's beautiful daughter, when Autumn was reminded of that terrible time.

She squatted before the child and smoothed back her dark hair. "I'm honored you have such faith in me, sweetie. I'm sorry you don't get along better with your mom, but I'm sure she loves you very much and wouldn't trade you for the world." Autumn plucked at the top button of Chloe's shirt. "You know, if I ever had a daughter, I'd want her to be just like you: beautiful, smart, and kind. You're the perfect trifecta," she said with a wide smile.

Chloe's pride couldn't be contained. It glowed from her like pure sunshine.

"Run along. Don't let my lazy sister oversleep, okay?"

"Okay."

As soon as Chloe cleared the door, the smile dropped from Autumn's face. Maintaining the cheerful demeanor took more than she could muster. She swallowed convulsively.

Crap! She experienced the very real fear that she might lose it in front of Keaton.

Without bothering to spare him a glance, she said, "Excuse me. I need a break."

FOR THE SECOND TIME THAT MORNING, KEATON WATCHED AUTUMN attempt to flee. But on this occasion, it was impossible to let her escape. Knowing she could send him to the farthest reaches of Alaska with a flick of her wrist, he stepped in her path all the same. His hands cupped her rigid jaw, and he dipped his head to force her to acknowledge him. "Autumn."

"Let me go, Keaton. I need..." She stopped speaking to take in huge gulps of air.

If he didn't know better, he'd think she was having a panic attack.

"Babe? What's going on? Talk to me."

Her head swung back and forth like an out-of-control pendulum. "I can't."

"You can. Tell me."

One slender hand came up to rest on her lower abdomen. "I was reminded of something I lost," she softly said.

He had to strain to hear her.

"My baby."

Autumn had been pregnant with another man's child.

Keaton's body went cold, then hot, and back to cold again. He dropped his hands as if burned. The proper thing would be to offer up condolences, yet the knowledge filled him with irrational rage. Over the years, he'd rejected the idea of her moving on or finding a lover. Logic said she wouldn't remain loyal to him, but he couldn't bring himself to think about her with someone else.

"Whose?" It slipped out before he could recall the word.

She stared at him in confusion for the span of four or five heartbeats. Understanding dawned. Something akin to hatred flashed on her face. "Nobody."

His brows hit his hairline. "Immaculate conception?" he scoffed, no longer caring to hide his anger and jealousy.

"You're something else, you know that?" she snapped. "You tossed me away like yesterday's news. What gives you the right to ask me anything?"

"Why won't you say? Was it one of my cousins?" The next thought had him fighting back the burning bile in the back of his throat. "Cooper?"

"Cooper?" she practically screeched the name. The pitch surely had dogs in the general vicinity howling in response. "Are you *insane*?"

Not C.C. then. Relieved, he nevertheless had to ask, "Zane? Knox?"

"The only Carlyle I've ever slept with was you, more the pity for me."

He had the distinct feeling he was missing something. "When?"

"When did I sleep with you? You were there, or was I that easy to forget? Oh, wait, yeah, I was. You moved on to Diane that same night you broke up with me."

Exhausted by the constant guilt and heartache, he said, "I thought you didn't want to talk about it, but hey, if you're ready to go there, let's do this thing."

The life seemed to drain from her. "I don't want to, Keaton. I'm tired of it all. Why do you think I left? Can we just work on your last task for today? I want to go home."

If he pushed, he'd be the biggest ass. But, he needed her to know he had truly loved her. That he had been devastated to think maybe she'd used magic to attract him and none of it had been real.

But her bitterness was well-founded.

The one thing bothering him now was the pregnancy. Why had he never heard rumor of it or the miscarriage? The only time she'd left town was in the days following their breakup.

His mind went blank and his face numb. Forming words was difficult. "Was it mine?" he finally managed to choke out.

She raised dull, brown eyes to stare at him.

He read the answer and nearly doubled over with the pain of loss. "Oh, babe."

"It's for the best," she said tightly. "I've changed my mind. I'm calling it a day."

"We need to talk about this," he insisted.

"No, Keaton. We really don't. What does it change?" She ran a shaky hand over her face and through her hair. "*Nothing*. It changes nothing. The facts remain; we broke up, you slept with Diane, you got her pregnant, you married her. We can't turn back time, and neither of us would want to." Her soft, sad smile broke his heart. "You have an amazing little girl, and I had a valuable life lesson about trust."

Tears blurred his vision. He wouldn't trade one for the other, but he would go to his grave mourning the loss of their unborn baby. "I know I ruined everything. And for that, I can never say how sorry I am."

"This is why I never told you. What good would it have done for you to feel the guilt and pain of what never was?"

"Any other woman—"

"I'm not," she snapped. "I'm not any other woman. I don't deal in what ifs or long for things I won't have. I live for here and now and, hopefully, a pleasant tomorrow. Anything else is a waste of time. Now, if you'll excuse me. I have business to attend."

Before she could brush past him, he hauled her into his arms. She struggled, but he held tight. "I know you could turn me into a cinder right now, but I'm hoping you'll give me a second to process this. While I do, I need to hold you."

She ceased her fight and dropped her arms to her sides.

He noted the balled fists and almost snorted.

This Autumn was far different than the girl of twenty-two he'd known and loved. That young woman had been open and caring. She had a smile for one and all. Every second of every day was a joy to be around her.

The woman who he held in his arms today was hard, cold, and bitter although she would claim otherwise. The outlook of the Autumn before him was jaded. Two months ago, he wouldn't have spared her the time of day. But he hadn't known what she'd been through. The loss she suffered.

"Does your family know about the baby?"

He guessed her response before she answered. "What was the point?" they said in unison.

"How could you go through that alone?" he whispered achingly.

42

She gave her standard careless shrug. "You know the saying. 'We're born alone, we live alone, we die alone.'"

"But I believe the remainder of that quote is 'Only through love and friendship can we create the illusion for the moment that we're not alone'."

"The key word is illusion, Keaton. Life, love, and friendship are only illusions. You and Diane taught me that."

"I loved you, Autumn."

She pulled away. "No, you were obsessed due to a spell, remember?"

He was sure he'd have come up with a clever denial, but she never gave him the chance. He blinked, and she was gone. To her Maine home was his assumption.

Christ, his chest ached. Today had been one contradicting moment after another with her.

She had defended his daughter at the diner then kissed him like there was no tomorrow. After delivering a kiss that damn near burned his socks off, she turned around and sailed out the door as if she didn't have a care in the world.

When Alastair threatened him, she lost her temper and attacked. Yet in the next breath, she denied caring about him anymore.

Their second kiss in less than an hour had her clinging to him like ivy.

Ten minutes later, she'd practically shoved a box of old mementos in his arms in her effort to be rid of the memories and him.

Ten minutes after *that*, she was training him in a cold and calculated manner alongside his daughter and brother.

But he suspected the real Autumn lay in the middle of the contradictions. The woman whose once-brilliant eyes had lost their shine. The woman who, for years, kept the truth hidden about a pregnancy and miscarriage because she didn't want the man she supposedly hated to have regrets or guilt for his dumbass actions.

Keaton sat down where he'd stood, too emotionally spent to move. One thing was true; he'd never gotten over her. The light citrus scent of her auburn hair, the smoothness of her silky skin, the taste of her wicked mouth—all still the same. All part of the formula that kept him awake nights. All part of the spectacular woman who'd been the ghost between him and Diane the four long years of their rocky marriage. The whole relationship had been a damned sham.

"Daddy?"

He answered automatically without opening his eyes. "Yeah, midget?"

"Where did Miss Autumn go?"

"I believe she might've gone home for the day."

"I like her. She never yells at me." The "like mommy" wasn't said, but it was definitely implied. "I wish she were my mom."

He opened his arms without a word, and she tumbled into his lap. How could he say he wished Autumn were her mom, too?

CHAPTER 6

*W*hen Keaton and Chloe entered the kitchen fifteen minutes later, he was surprised to see Autumn at the table. In front of her was the largest cinnamon roll he'd ever seen. The damned thing was as wide as the dinner plate it sat on.

Unexpected laughter escaped. She'd always had a healthy appetite and loved all things sweet. "You plan on eating that whole thing?"

"I'm going to give it the old college try," she said as she ripped off another chunk and dipped it into a large bowl of icing.

"We were getting ready to head out. Thanks for everything today."

She glanced up, and their eyes connected across the small space. With her chin, she nodded to the chairs across from her. "If you're not in a hurry, you should have one of Winnie's rolls."

Keaton almost stuck his index finger in his ear and wiggled to make sure his hearing was intact. Had she invited him to stay and share food? His shock must've been apparent because she smirked.

"I'm not that much of a bi... uh, wench," she corrected with a soft smile for Chloe.

He helped Chloe into her seat and selected one for himself

directly opposite Autumn. "I don't think you're that much of a bi… wench at all." He was deliberate with his words and offered up a smile.

A little of the haunted look left her eyes. Or maybe it was his imagination, and he only wanted her to be happier.

She shoved the food to the center of the table and handed them each a fork from the pile there. "Dig in. Don't let me be the only glutton."

When the first bite of cinnamon goodness hit his tongue, Keaton's eyes rolled back in his head. "Dear gawd! This is fantastic," he said around the mouthful.

"Right?! That's what I'm sayin'." Autumn turned her warm gaze on Chloe. "What do you think, kid? Good?"

Chloe's wide grin triggered Keaton's.

"You know what's even better?" Autumn's smile was full of deviltry. "Ice cream!"

"For breakfast?" Chloe asked, awestruck.

"What better time?" Autumn asked, as she stood and brushed by Keaton to get to the freezer. "We have vanilla and triple chocolate chunk. Oh, and moose tracks. What is your guilty pleasure, Chloe, my dear?"

"Vanilla, please, Miss Autumn."

"Keaton? Are you still into vanilla after all this time?"

"Yep. Make mine a double scoop."

"Daddy!"

"It's Autumn's idea," he defended. "I'm only getting behind it."

"Then let's be real rebels and eat from the carton," Autumn laughed and plunked the container next to the roll. "Last one to the bottom is an elephant turd."

"An Eddie elephant turd!" Chloe piped up, referring to the resident rescue in Summer's Sanctuary.

As Autumn interacted with his daughter, Keaton experienced a sense of what family life would've been like for them had he not lost his mind in the glen. A deep longing, along with "what if", tormented him. All he'd ever wanted was a loving family like he had growing up. He'd never had exceptional goals and was content to live life as it came. Keaton hadn't grown up with dreams of being anything but normal and staid.

"Miss Autumn, you should marry my dad and be my mom."

Both Keaton and Autumn froze with their spoons halfway to their mouths.

She cast him a helpless glance, and because he wanted to hear her field the underlying question, he remained silent.

Without breaking eye contact with him, she said, "That's not possible." A couple of heartbeats passed before she faced his daughter and gentled her voice. "Two people should only marry if they love each other."

"But you kissed my dad two times. Doesn't that mean you love him?"

The shade of Autumn's face turned the color of a ripe tomato.

He could feel the warmth building under his skin too. *The little sneak!* Apparently, she *had* witnessed the second kiss. Keaton had to remember to engage the eyes in the back of his head from here on out.

Autumn recovered her speech. With her spoon, she gestured toward the treats on the table. "Eat your ice cream."

"Smooth," he murmured.

When she shot him the stink eye, he laughed.

Although they weren't together, Keaton found himself experiencing a deep happiness. As if, in this moment with these two people, he was where he was supposed to be. He took a heaping spoonful of ice cream and closed his eyes to savor the moment.

When he opened them, Autumn's solemn gaze was focused on him again. He was unable to blink, unable to break their spontaneous connection.

What did she see when she looked at him now? A Class-A idiot? Because that's what he felt like to have let go of someone as magnificent as Autumn.

Laughter echoed in the foyer, and Autumn turned toward the sound. Coop and Summer arrived hand-in-hand, practically glowing with joy. Their blissfulness soured Keaton's stomach. He didn't begrudge them their love, but he was over-the-top envious and had yet to find a way to come to grips with it.

"Ice cream? For breakfast?" Coop inquired with a raised brow.

"It was Miss Autumn's idea," Chloe volunteered.

Autumn compressed her lips, but the dimple in her cheek was a clear testament to her amusement. "Thanks for throwing me under the bus, kid. Besides, it's now considered brunch since we've been up for hours, right?"

Autumn licked the remaining ice cream from her spoon. Desire hit Keaton where it counted. The sight of her tongue twisting around the curve of the metal utensil brought back sensual memories of the two of them that were best forgotten. He could easily recall the things she could do with her agile tongue. Sweat broke out on his forehead.

"Daddy, are you okay? Why do you look sick?"

All eyes turned to him. A knowing light flared to life in Autumn's gaze, and for a brief second, mischief lightened her irises to a shade closer to the warm amber he remembered.

"I think it was too much sugar, midget." Coop's save was well-timed and appreciated. "You know how your dad gets when he has too many sweets."

Autumn rose to clear the table. "Thanks for sharing my breakfast. But I need to discuss important adult things with my sisters." She laid a free hand on Chloe's dark head. "Think about what you might want to try for tomorrow's lesson. Maybe, if it's not outrageous, we can give it a whirl. What do you say?"

"You're the best, Miss Autumn."

"Since we have bonded over ice cream, you can drop the Miss and just call me Autumn. That's a mouthful as it is."

Chloe beamed and blossomed under the attention.

"I'd like Coop and Keaton to stay for the discussion," Summer said.

Autumn froze with the freezer door open. "Summer." She said her sister's name in warning.

"I'm not keeping secrets from Coop," Summer said stubbornly. "And I think Keaton might have something to contribute."

A concerned frown creased Autumn's brow. She cut a side glance Chloe's way and then toward Keaton before she nodded to her sister. "Fine."

"I'll text Knox to see if he can help Chloe with her studies today," Keaton said.

"I already did," Coop said. "Summer also messaged Spring to join us."

The sound of multiple cars on the drive caught Keaton's attention.

"Right on schedule. That should be Knox and Spring," Coop predicted.

Raised voices streamed through the open window.

"You drive like a maniac!" Knox charged and slammed his truck door.

"It's better than driving like a ninety-year-old grandma," Spring retorted.

The four adults in the kitchen rushed to the window for a better view of the unfolding drama.

"I've never heard Spring raise her voice," Keaton murmured in Autumn's ear.

She scooted closer to him as Chloe wiggled into the mass of adults. "That's because my sister doesn't lose her temper. It makes this an interesting development."

He laughed and rested a hand on her waist to balance them both as he leaned forward.

Spring gasped and then screeched. "You're a jackass!"

"Better than a—" Knox choked and gagged, cutting off the remainder of his words.

"What do you suppose she did to him?" Coop whispered.

"If I had to guess, a mouthful of dirt," Autumn responded, careful to keep her voice down. "She did that to me once when I yelled at her. Spring doesn't like anyone to disrupt her Zen."

"If he didn't know what we were before this morning. He does now," Summer predicted.

"We had a conversation yesterday when he returned," Keaton told her. "He's known all along."

"What?" both sisters cried in unison, forgetting to keep their voices down.

"He's always known he's a warlock and that you're witches. He's been practicing magic from birth." Keaton shrugged. "How we never picked up on it is beyond me."

Autumn grunted and faced the window, but the duo outside had moved inside and were glaring from the kitchen door.

"Oh, hey." Summer offered up a sickly smile and a wave. "We didn't know you guys had arrived."

Spring scoffed her disbelief, sat down, and peeled off a chunk of cinnamon roll.

"Uh, Spring, you're dripping wet," Autumn pointed out. "Should I get you a towel?"

As if just noticing her wrecked appearance, Spring glanced down. With a glare in Knox's direction, she waved her hands and restored herself to the dry, pristine state she'd been in when she left that morning. "Someone thought it would be funny to dump one of my flower arrangements over my head."

"Someone thought it would be funny to fill my mouth with dirt," Knox countered with a return scowl.

"You were being ugly," Spring yelled.

"Children, children!" Autumn laughed. "Let's set a better example for the actual child in the group, huh?"

Knox scraped his knuckles over his tongue and grimaced. "Yeah," he agreed, but his look promised retribution for her sister. He addressed Coop with his next statement. "Zane is following in another few minutes. He said, since it's Saturday, he doesn't mind watching Chloe. I thought maybe another mind to help figure out a solution might be needed."

"Should've given us the smart one. Zane would be a much better contributor than *you*," Spring stated and primly dipped a small piece of cinnamon roll into the frosting.

Before she could consume it, the piece flew across the room and landed in Knox's mouth. His grin was as obnoxious as his chewing.

Keaton crossed his arms and settled back against the sink where Autumn still stood. "I've never seen him like this. This is better than a TV drama."

AUTUMN GIGGLED. A LARGE PART OF HER KNEW SHE SHOULDN'T encourage Keaton's playful side, but like she'd told him, she was tired of the fighting. If they maintained the cease-fire and shared a friendly moment on occasion, she'd consider the time with him well-spent.

Another vehicle entered the drive, and she twisted to see. "Looks like Zane has arrived."

Chloe pouted. "I don't want to go home."

Before Keaton could speak, Autumn squatted in front of the child. "Afraid to miss all the fun, kid?"

Chloe nodded, pout still firmly in place.

"I'll tell you what. If it's all right with your father, I'll swing by later today. We'll get pedicures, and I'll fill you in on any juicy details."

The girl cast her father a pleading look. "Daddy?"

The pause dragged on so long, Autumn twisted her upper body to face him.

His eyes burned with unnamed emotion.

Her heart pinged in reaction, but she was quick to shut it down. That way lay more heartache. She wouldn't go there.

Keaton nodded wordlessly.

"Thank you!" Chloe yelled her delight.

"If you don't mind company, we can make it a girls' day," Spring directed to Chloe.

"Yes, it could be fun. Like a secret witches' society," Summer said with a laugh.

Chloe's honey-colored eyes rounded in awe. "I can be part of your club?"

"Sweetie, you will be our honorary president," Autumn told her.

She should've been better prepared for the impact of the little body against hers, but the enthusiastic hug knocked her on her ass and into Keaton's legs.

"I've never had a pedicure before," Chloe said in a wobbly voice.

"If you cry, I might start. We could flood this kitchen in no time," Autumn warned with a last squeeze before climbing to her feet with an assist from Keaton and Chloe. "And I imagine it's because you've lived with the guys. Boys are dumb and don't realize what a woman needs. Pedicures and pampering being top of the list, of course."

"Word!" Spring added. "I think Winnie has some new lotions she wants to try out. Maybe we can convince her to let us explore her shop before we go."

Chloe's excitement could scarcely be contained. Autumn could hear her chatting all the way to Zane's sporty car.

"Should we have Holly pop over for the meeting?" Summer asked.

Since she'd found her long-lost twin, Summer had been quick to include their other sister in all things family related. None of the Thorne sisters minded because Holly was a breath of fresh air and a welcome addition to their family.

"Works for me." Autumn put on water to boil for tea. "Now let's get down to business. The Chintamani Stone and mother. I don't trust Alastair as far as I can throw him. This morning, he threatened to hurt Keaton if I didn't do what he wanted."

"That's his M.O. But I don't believe he would really do it," Summer demurred as she typed out a text.

"Believe it, sister. He will be ruthless to get what he wants," Autumn assured her as she prepped her drink and brewed a carafe of coffee for the others. She pointed out the fact that Alastair had recently tried to take a chimpanzee from Summer's care. "Didn't he come for Morty not that long ago? I think the only reason he played nice is because he's trying to impress you, Summer. The new father thing and all that. But don't think for a minute he wouldn't steamroll over the rest of us."

Winnie arrived for the last of Autumn's statement. "I agree."

Summer appeared frustrated, and for that, Autumn had a twinge of conscience, but she wouldn't risk her life to please her sister's need to bring Alastair into the fold.

"However, I'm inclined to go after the stone anyway," Autumn added, much to the surprise of those around her. "I know I said I didn't think he should have it, and I still believe it's too powerful for him to possess. But if there is a chance he's correct and it can save Mom, then I'm going for it."

Winnie held up a piece of paper filled with her notes. "I don't think it will be as easy as we originally thought."

"Pfft. It never is," Autumn muttered. In a louder voice, she asked, "What's the problem?"

"First, the monks. You're a woman. I don't know that they will give you the time of day. The cluster where the Roerichs were headed is old school and private," Winnie explained. "In reading more of Helena's diary, I'm convinced that had her husband not been with her, she wouldn't have gained their cooperation in hiding the stone."

Autumn made a face. "What's the other problem? Or is there more than just the two?"

"Yeah, remember when we discussed the couple theory?" The sisters nodded as one. "Well, I think you were right about the note in the margin."

"Dammit!" The hits kept coming.

All the men looked adorably confused. Keaton was the first to interrupt the discussion under way. "What is this stone, why is it in a monastery, what does it have to do with your mother, and why is it too powerful for your uncle to own?"

Autumn clapped her hands in a slow steady beat. "I'm impressed with how well you were paying attention." She shared a speaking glance with her sisters before she replied. "The Chintamani Stone is rumored to grant wishes to the person who possesses it." She took a sip of tea before continuing. "Its last known whereabouts was referenced in a diary by Helena Roerich. She and her husband were the safe keepers of the stone. But rumor about the power they held spread like wildfire, and interest in the stone went off the charts. They had to find a place to stash it to prevent it from falling into the wrong hands."

Summer finished the explanation, "Alastair believes he can bring our mother out of stasis if he has ownership of it. He's convinced the stone is at a monastery in the Himalayan mountains. We..." She gestured to her group of sisters. "...believe we've narrowed it down to China."

Winnie placed a map in the center of the table and pointed to a small town. "This village is the closest to the one Helena described in her diary, but it's not the name of the town she originally stated."

"Summer told me y'all believe this stone has to be retrieved by a couple," Coop interrupted. "While I don't understand exactly why, I'm willing to go with her to retrieve it."

"No," Autumn said. "We discussed this. Summer's magic backfires, and you aren't experienced enough to help her. Remember your little attempt to learn on your own? The squirrel mafia tried to off poor Eddie."

"Then what do *you* suggest?" Summer asked irritably.

"I'm the strongest witch with the exception of Winnie. I'll head to China for a scouting expedition after I wrap up a few things. Probably early next week. If I need help, I'll call."

Knox, who had been listening silently from his vantage point by the refrigerator, spoke up. "I suspect the couple issue comes in due to the initial legend surrounding the stone. It can drive the person possessing the stone to do terrible things. Love can temper its power."

"Makes sense. I'd be curious to discover more about it," Autumn replied.

"Yeah, some of those magic objects are fascinating." He smiled his understanding. "And I can go with you. I'm the most experienced warlock of our line."

"Absolutely not," Keaton objected.

All occupants of the kitchen turned their shocked gazes on him, but it was Autumn's gaze he met and held. Was he jealous at the idea of her spending time with his cousin?

"Care to tell me why not?" Knox asked, amusement heavy in his voice.

Keaton scowled. "Look at you. You're a damned Greek God. I don't want her anywhere near you."

"You act as if you have a say in what I do, Keaton," Autumn laughed harshly. "You don't."

His mouth opened and closed a few times as he struggled with what he intended to say. He didn't have a chance to respond before they were interrupted by the arrival of Holly and Quentin, Holly's self-appointed bodyguard.

All the women sighed in stereo as he stepped fully into the room, their eyes glued to various parts of his anatomy encased in his tight muscle t-shirt and black jeans.

"Who the hell are *you*?" Keaton demanded.

"Quentin Buchanan," all the women said at once.

Quentin's grin flashed. It was lopsided in nature but promised naughty things to come. Autumn's ovaries stood up and took notice.

CHAPTER 7

*I*f Keaton thought his cousin looked like a Greek God, it went doubly so for the stranger who stepped into the kitchen. The newcomer topped Keaton's six-foot-three by another few inches and took up the remaining space in the Thornes' tiny kitchen. Together with the shoulder-length dark hair, the cocky grin, and dark, hooded eyes, the man was sex on a stick.

Keaton disliked him on sight.

His ire spiked higher as he witnessed the lust enter the eyes of every woman present. Autumn had yet to take her gaze from the preening peacock. She dropped her chin in her palm and sighed.

A quick glance at the other Carlyle men showed Keaton's hostility wasn't misplaced. They all sensed this guy posed a threat. If testosterone had a smell, it would overwhelm and suffocate the inhabitants of the room.

When Quentin met his cold stare and winked, Keaton nearly came out of his chair. The fucker knew what he was doing.

"What, you wearing some magical pheromone cologne or something?" Keaton asked. Disdain dripped from his words.

The bastard had the nerve to laugh. Christ, even his belly laugh was sexy. Yep, Keaton definitely hated him.

Knox chuckled and was the first to offer his hand.

"Someone snap a pic," Autumn said. "I need this for cold nights in Maine."

"You can have me for cold nights in Maine, gorgeous," Quentin had the nerve to respond.

"That's going to be awfully difficult when I rip off your junk and stuff it up your ass," Keaton growled.

All heads spun his way with varying degrees of shock or amusement. The last being Quentin. Obviously, he didn't feel Keaton was a threat.

"I don't mind cuddling instead. Whatever the women want, dude," the guy had the nerve to say.

Autumn's sexy, musical laugh—the one Keaton hadn't heard in years—rang out and socked him in the gut. He wanted to swear a blue streak.

It was Holly who backhanded Quentin in his rock-hard abs and ordered, "Knock it off, Romeo. We have work to do."

"I'm an excellent multitasker," Quentin said. "You'd know that if only you'd let me—"

She clamped a hand over his grinning mouth, and her face turned the color of a beet. "Shut it," she hissed. "It's never happening."

Quentin removed her hand, but not before dropping a kiss onto her palm. "Keep telling yourself that, my love."

"Be a sport and take one for the team, Holly. Then that sonofabitch will stop ogling my woman," Coop said.

"Sorry to be a buzzkill, man, but I'll always ogle the women. It's like saying an artist isn't allowed to appreciate a masterpiece."

"Oh, I think he just called me a masterpiece," Summer sighed.

Coop pulled her to his side and dropped a kiss on her lips. "You're *my* masterpiece, but you're remaining in my private collection."

She giggled and snuggled close. "Sweet talker."

Keaton nearly gagged at all the sexual vibes floating around the room. To redirect the conversation, he tapped the map. "Can we get back to the subject at hand? The damned stone."

Autumn stood and suggested they all adjourn to the living room where there was more seating. "I'll brew more coffee."

Quentin stepped forward. "I'll help."

Outraged, Keaton surged to his feet and, in the process, sent his chair skittering across the wood floor into the cabinets. "If anyone is *helping* her, it's me."

The other man's lips twisted into a mocking half-smile. "It's only coffee, man, but if you need to get territorial about the brew, I get it."

Violence—cold, swift, and deadly—danced between the two men.

The warm touch of Autumn's palm as she cupped Keaton's chin, snapped him out of his caveman attitude. He allowed her to turn his head while his eyes still blazed a warning at Quentin.

"Keaton," she said softly. Their gazes connected. "Enough."

Her fingers lightly stroked along his jawline and brought the tightened muscles there to his attention. With an effort, he unclenched his jaw and stopped grinding his teeth.

"He's a flirt. Nothing more," she assured him.

"I'm hurt. You might as well have castrated me and put me out to pasture, darlin'," Quentin complained, hand over his heart.

"Not a bad idea," Keaton snapped.

The other man grinned and touched two fingers to his forehead before he swept from the room.

"He's awesome eye candy, but he might as well have Holly's name tattooed on his forehead," Autumn said with a light laugh. "Watch and you'll see; he is never far from her side. And she's the only one he ever calls 'my love'."

Keaton studied Autumn for a full minute as she removed mugs from the cabinet and scooped grounds into the coffee filter. "You didn't have to ease my mind. Why did you?"

She shrugged. "Maybe I don't like bloodshed in the kitchen."

"I think we need to deal with whatever is still between us."

"And what is that, Keaton? A residual feeling of jealousy and distrust?"

58

"I think it's more along the lines of this," he said and pulled her into his arms.

He paused long enough to make sure she wanted his kiss then lowered his lips to hers. When he met with no resistance from her, his tongue dipped into the warm hollow of her mouth.

Her arms came up, and her fingers twisted into the hair at the base of his neck. Her little moan of pleasure shot straight to his groin. Keaton couldn't get enough. Her taste nearly sent him over the edge of reason.

"Oh! Sorry," Spring chirped from somewhere behind them.

He heard the shuffle of feet to indicate she'd left.

In slow stages, Keaton and Autumn detangled from one another, but their gazes remained locked. "Go out to dinner with me tomorrow night," he asked, his voice heavy with want and need.

"Should we go down that rabbit hole again, Keaton?" she asked softly.

"I'd follow you anywhere, Alice."

"Oh, fuck. That was totally romantic," she griped. "How do I say no to that?"

Laughter overtook him, and she joined in. It was the second time she allowed herself to be carefree in his presence, and he reveled in it. He wasn't lying when he'd told her he missed the girl he'd known. She'd been fresh and fun without trying.

"Is that a yes?"

"I'm going to regret this."

"Not if I can help it," he assured her.

"Go. Give me a minute to gather my thoughts."

Keaton leaned down and captured her mouth in a light, clinging kiss. "Does that mean my sex appeal scatters your thoughts?"

"It means you boggle the brain. Go! And take these mugs with you. I'll bring out the coffee and creamer."

AFTER HE'D GONE, AUTUMN SANK DOWN INTO THE NEAREST CHAIR. *What the hell had she agreed to?* Today she intended to spend time with his kid, and tomorrow night she'd scheduled dinner with Keaton. Goddess, she was already in deeper than she should be.

She'd been telling the truth when she said he boggled the brain. He totally did. By the time they'd finished a conversation, she didn't know if she was coming or going. All she *did* know was that she wanted him with an intensity that could never be assuaged. No one else had the ability to ease the ache in her soul.

Yet every time they were together, old hurts resurfaced.

Keaton seemed to be dealing with those hurts better than she, but then again, he wasn't the truly injured party. She had been. Did she dare give him a second chance to ravage her heart?

If, by some miracle of the Goddess, they did end up back together, how could Autumn bear to deal with Diane on a continuous basis? Diane was a constant in his life as was his daughter—*the constant reminder of the child Autumn had lost.*

"The coffee's been done for five minutes."

Autumn caught back her surprised scream. "Goddess! Way to terrify me!"

Knox grinned and shoved away from the wall he'd been leaning against. "I have a good idea, but what are you thinking about so hard?"

"What else?"

"Are you going to give him a second chance?"

"That's what I was working through. There's a lot of leftover baggage."

"If I go to China with you, he'll lose his shit," Knox warned then ruined it with a wicked grin. "I would pay good money to see it."

"Who knew you had a mean streak?"

He sidled up to her and cupped her cheek. "I prefer to think of myself as devilish."

"Devilishly handsome," she teased.

"If only you'd looked at me first," he said with a mock sigh.

"Hmm, didn't you say something similar to Summer?"

Knox laughed. "I might have."

Autumn shifted to prepare a tray. "What was the deal with you and Spring earlier?"

His open, friendly expression disappeared. "She's a menace."

"Are we talking about the same woman? My sister is as easy going as they come."

"Or so she'd like you to believe."

"What aren't you telling me, Knox? Did something happen between you?"

"No, and in spite of her attempts, nothing will," he said and smoothly lifted the tray from her hands. "Lead the way so I can watch your ass."

"Should I add an extra wiggle?"

"Please do."

She loved their easy banter. Knox had the ability to take her mind from the stressful side of life. She figured it must be his calm, carefree energy. Not much fazed him—*with the exception of her little sister apparently.*

Once everyone was settled in the living room and had coffee in hand, discussion of the Chintamani Stone began in earnest.

"I can rearrange some things and leave for China as early as the day after tomorrow," Autumn said. She held up a hand to forestall any argument from the crowd after she said, "And I go alone."

She shouldn't have wasted the energy to lift her arm.

As the discussion circled around who would go with her, Keaton remained quiet.

She arched a brow. His eyes spoke volumes, and his warm grin made her smile. In that second, the knowledge he was meant to go with her whispered through her mind. "Keaton's going with me," she said, never taking her gaze from his. "Tomorrow I'll see he has the basics of magic down just in case."

"What about your mayoral duties?" Coop asked him.

"I'm due a vacation," Keaton said with an unconcerned air. "My staff can handle anything that pops up this week."

"Why him?" Quentin asked, his dark, bedroom eyes curious.

Autumn rose and placed a hand on Keaton's shoulder. Once she touched him, she felt him relax from the challenge. "Because he speaks the Tibetan language and doesn't rub people the wrong way."

Coop's lower jaw hit his chest. "Dude! Seriously? How did I not know this?"

Keaton shrugged. "I learned after college." He covered Autumn's hand with his. "Once upon a time, Autumn and I thought about taking a trip to Tibet."

"Anyway, he speaks the language, and I don't," Autumn stated matter-of-factly. "I think he'll be helpful in communicating." She cast a regretful look at Quentin. "No disrespect intended, but I don't know you, and I don't trust you aren't in Alastair's pocket."

Quentin's randy expression disappeared and was replaced by a grudging respect. "Fair enough."

Knox held up a finger to gain everyone's attention. "Since Coop first mentioned it to me, I've done a bit of research on my own. Alastair isn't going to be able to bring Aurora back without a bit of help. Not only does he need the assist of six witches, preferably of the same powerful family line, he'll also need another artifact or, more correctly, three."

"Your mother's name was Aurora?" Quentin asked with a laugh. "As in Sleeping Beauty? Talk about the irony."

Holly elbowed Quentin and responded to Knox. "There are five daughters of Aurora. With Alastair to oversee the ceremony, that essentially gives us six witches. He only needs one more. But if it needs to be her blood relation, we can try to contact her brother, Trace."

"There's still the matter of the next piece of the puzzle," Knox said.

Spring, who had been mostly silent until now, asked him, "Which is?"

Knox pointedly avoided her and sauntered across the room to refill his coffee mug. "The original Mjölnir amulet."

"Thor's hammer," Spring said.

Knox stopped mid-pour to gape at her.

"While I don't have a genius IQ in the one-fifty range like you, I'm not as dumb as you seem to think I am," she snapped.

Autumn tamped down her laughter. While their whole family possessed above average intelligence, Spring was the smartest of all the Thorne sisters with an IQ of one-forty-nine.

Spring went on to explain the myth surrounding the amulet. "In addition to being the God of thunder and lightning, Thor was the God of healing and fertility. The original amulet's setting houses a stone from Odin's ring and was blessed by Thor himself. The runes on the amulet contain a spell for healing." She took a dainty sip of her coffee. "It's also said whoever possesses the amulet has the power to heal anyone or anything."

"Then why would Alastair even need the Chintamani Stone if he could get his hands on the amulet?" Autumn asked.

"Knox, would you like to field that one?" Spring asked with a saccharine-infused sweetness in her smile.

"But you're doing so well," he replied with an equally false smile.

"If you insist." She addressed the room and said, "Based on a conversation I happened to overhear between our father and Knox—"

Knox scoffed. "Happened to overhear? You mean spied on. But do continue."

Spring shot him the glare of death. "As I was saying before I was so rudely interrupted, based on a conversation between Knox and Dad, the spell they believe Alastair intends to use requires four artifacts. The Chintamani Stone, the Mjölnir amulet, an Egyptian Uterine amulet that contains similar runes to the Mjölnir amulet, and an ancient Greek scroll last known to be in da Vinci's possession." She twisted to look at Knox. "Oh, and just why were you meeting with my father in the first place?"

"None of your damned business," he retorted.

"You must like the taste of dirt," she snapped.

"In essence, you're saying going after these items is a wild goose chase," Quentin stated in disgust, preventing World War III from erupting in the Thorne living room.

"Pretty much," Knox confirmed.

Summer leaned forward and set her cup down. "We did suspect the other items were needed, but why hasn't Alastair mentioned these other things to us?"

"I don't know. Perhaps he feels his magic is strong enough to pull off a healing with just the Chintamani Stone. Or it could be that he already has the other three objects. There's really no way to know unless you ask him." Knox shrugged and finished off the last of his coffee. "On that note, I have to run, but you have my number if you need me." He leaned in and kissed Autumn's cheek. "Safe travels."

CHAPTER 8

*S*ummer rounded on Autumn in disbelief. *"You agreed to let Keaton go to China with you?"*

The door had just closed behind the last of the Carlyle men, and Quentin had wandered off into the kitchen to scavenge for food.

"Shhh! They haven't left yet," Autumn hissed.

Spring shot back the peephole to watch. The sound of slamming doors preceded her signal for the all clear. "Spill," she said.

"Y'all are making more of it than there is," Autumn hedged.

"I'mma call bullshit on that one," Spring laughed. "I saw you kissing in the kitchen."

"*What?*" Summer practically screeched. "You were kissing Keaton."

Face flaming, Autumn headed down the hall. "I don't answer to any of you."

Like a gaggle of ducks, the sisters fell in line behind her.

"Was it as good as you remember?" Winnie asked dreamily.

"It sure as hell looked like it," Spring volunteered with a short laugh.

"Is this wise?" Summer ran to catch up.

Autumn stopped short, and one by one, her sisters crashed into one another. "Enough!"

She spun to face the group and moderated her tone. "Enough. Yes, I kissed Keaton. More than once. Yes, it was as good as I remember. Better. No, it isn't wise, but I couldn't seem to help myself." She heaved a heavy sigh. "And before anyone else asks, I'm not ready to start something again. I'm only having dinner with him tomorrow night. If it goes south, then I'll rethink taking him to China. Happy?"

Their expressions ranged from concerned to cynical to delighted. Autumn ignored them all. "Can we please clean the living room and get ready for our pedicures. I'll call Dixie and see if we can book the entire salon for late afternoon. Does that work for everyone?"

A chorus of "yes" answered her.

"Good. Winnie, can you fill in and train Coop and Chloe while I'm gone?"

"Yep."

"Perfect. Any other questions?" Autumn asked.

No one answered, and she followed the sightline of their gazes to the kitchen. Quentin stood shirtless scrubbing dishes.

"Holy shit!" she breathed. "How is it possible for one man to be so perfect?"

"He's hardly perfect," Holly snapped. "Put your eyes back into your heads and roll up your tongues, ladies."

"Sorry." Autumn gave her a one-armed hug. "I realize you must get women lusting over your man a lot."

"He's not my man!"

"Riiiiiight. You're a Thorne, hon. You'll only love once. Might as well make it a good one."

"I was already in love," Holly reminded her. "It's a crock of shit." She sneezed, and within seconds, the squawking of birds could be heard outside the windows.

Mr. Black, Spring's raven familiar, glided down the stairs and landed on the railing with a caw.

Quentin charged into the hallway with a wicked-looking blade in hand. "What's going on? Who upset you?"

"Who says I'm upset?" Holly demanded irritably.

"The Alfred Hitchcock scene outside the window," he laughed and lowered his knife. "The birds only come when you swear. You only swear when you are extremely upset. So, I ask again, my love, who has you upset? I will sever his head from his body."

Summer meeped.

All eyes turned to her.

"I can't help it. It's so romantic," she said.

"You call it romantic. I call it overdramatic," Holly retorted.

"You should just give in and bang nasties with him," Winnie suggested with a dopey grin. "Then you can tell us how amazing he is. We won't have to wonder anymore."

"What is wrong with you people? You're a bunch of sex-starved bitches!" Holly raged, sneezed, and disappeared into thin air. The sound of birds pecking the living room window was ignored by all.

"Think we pissed her off by teasing her about you-know-who?" Summer asked.

All eyes turned to Quentin who lounged in the doorway.

"You ladies are a sight to behold," he said with an appreciative sigh. "But alas, I need to follow my prickly pear."

"Let us know what we can do to help wear her down." Autumn eyed his beautiful bare chest. "And feel free to clean our kitchen shirtless any time the urge strikes."

Heat stole into his cheeks as he glanced down. "Sorry, I didn't want to get my shirt dirty."

"I get the feeling he isn't as much of a playboy as he'd like people to believe," Autumn said after he'd left.

"I agree. I think he does it to piss off Holly," Summer said. "Doesn't mean we can't have fun with it. He keeps our guys on their toes."

"Our guys?" Spring asked. "Keaton and Coop maybe. But Winnie and I don't have 'guys' yet."

"Knox isn't your *guy*?" Autumn teased.

"Not hardly. He's an insufferable bore."

Autumn, Summer, and Winnie burst into laughter.

"Yeah, keep telling yourself that, sister. Maybe one day you'll believe it." Autumn kissed Spring on her pink cheek. "Word of advice? Start behaving as if you don't care. Maybe go out with someone else on occasion. It will drive him insane and bring him running."

"I don't play games," Spring said. Her chin lifted at a proud angle. "If he doesn't want me, fine. But I'm not going to be like all the other women in town."

Autumn urged Summer and Winnie to leave then faced Spring. "Time for the hard truth. You've spent the better part of the last six years displaying your wares for him—*just like the women of this town.*" She smoothed back Spring's dark-brown hair. "You're classier than that, sister. Knock it off."

Tears clouded her sister's wide green eyes. "His light is amazing. Something in me craves it."

"I know. I also know you are the most beautiful woman on the face of this green earth. You could own the world if you wished. But making yourself readily available to a man who can have any woman he wants is not the answer. Like all contrary men, he'll want what he has to work for."

Autumn wiped away the tears from Spring's pale, smooth cheeks. "In the meantime, buy a vibrator. It's worked for me for years."

"I... it's that... I never..." The fiery blush spread from Spring's neck to her hairline.

The realization hit. Autumn's mouth could catch flies, it opened so wide. "You're a *virgin?*"

"Shhh!"

"But you're twenty-five! No one is a virgin that late in life."

"Why don't you take out a page in the Williamson Herald while you're at it!" Spring snapped, referring to the local Leiper's Fork newspaper.

"Gurrllll! We need to do something about that. No wonder you're so testy lately. You should've lost that shit a long time ago."

"Well, I didn't have a willing participant like you and some of our other sisters," Spring said nastily.

"Oh, stop. You could snap your fingers and have any man ready to do the deed," Autumn said impatiently. "And you should. Get rid of that hindrance and get some experience. That way, when you finally hook up with *The One*, you have something to compare to."

Her sister gazed at her thoughtfully. "You think I should?"

"I do. Saving it for a man who may never want you is a great waste."

Spring nodded slowly. "I think you're right. What about Deputy Aimes?"

"Eww, no. He was with Carol Anne Connor, and she gave him herpes."

"How do you know these things?" Spring inquired.

"I know everything about this rinky-dink town. It's a curse and a blessing," Autumn smirked. "Make me a list of hot guys you find sexy. I'll help you screen them."

"You do know witches can't contract those types of diseases, right?" her sister reminded her.

"I know that, but the thought still makes me cringe inside. Didn't I just say he was with Carol Anne?" Autumn mock shuddered.

KEATON SHUFFLED THE PAPERS ON HIS DESK AND STARED AT THE print. Nothing penetrated his brain. His mind was occupied with thoughts of Autumn and all that had transpired today: the earth-shattering kisses, her acceptance of his dinner invitation, her offer to take Chloe for pedicures, and her acknowledgment that he might be the best candidate to go to China with her.

He smiled as he recalled the flashes of the girl he remembered. The teasing light had been back in her eyes. It made him heart-happy to witness the change since a huge part of him believed her unhappiness lay at his door.

A faint knock caught his attention. "Come in."

Chloe's tear-stained face appeared around the door.

Keaton surged to his feet and closed the distance between them. "What's wrong, sweetheart? Are you hurt?"

"No, Daddy." She lifted her arms for him to scoop her up.

"Why are you crying, Chloe? Did someone hurt your feelings?"

"Mama called me and said I can't go to get pedicures today," she sobbed into his shoulder.

He held her tight and rocked her at the same time he rubbed her back. "I'm not sure how she found out, but it's not up to your mother. You are in my care this weekend, and I say you can go."

She pulled back, all crying ceased. "Really?"

"Really."

Her large, solemn eyes filled again. "But she'll be mad."

"She'll get over it," he assured her.

Chloe bit her lip and ducked her head.

"What aren't you telling me, Chloe?"

"Nothing," she mumbled.

"Lying to me is not a good thing, sweetheart. You know that right? I can't help you if you lie."

Her little chest expanded and contracted as sobs wracked her body.

Keaton held her close and let her cry. With the feeling of helplessness came anger. It was well past time for him and Diane to have a sit down over her behavior toward their daughter. But in the meantime, he had to get to the root of Chloe's tears.

After her sobs calmed to sniffles, he carried her to the kitchen and sat her on the granite countertop by the sink.

The deep-seated knowledge settled in his chest that he wasn't going to like the truth. He tried to maintain a neutral expression for Chloe's sake.

He grabbed a clean dishtowel from the cabinet and ran it under cool water. After wringing out the excess water, he patted her swollen eyes then followed it up with a kiss of each lid.

"Feel better?"

She shrugged her shoulders, and the gesture was so like Autumn, he felt a pang in the region of his heart.

"Chloe, I'm going to ask you something, and I need the God's honest truth from you. Okay?"

She nodded, expression glum.

"Has your mother ever hurt you?"

Her lip quivered, and her eyes dropped to her purple-sequined tennis shoes.

"Chloe. Look at me."

She refused and shook her head emphatically.

It was obvious that something was seriously wrong, but he'd be damned if he knew how to get the truth from her.

"How old are you, Chloe?"

Her head whipped up, and the frown on her face was priceless. "You know I'm eight and a half."

"That's right. And would you say you're a big girl now?"

"Uh huh."

"I agree." He dropped a kiss on her nose and placed a finger under her chin to keep her gaze on his. "But big girls don't tell lies. They tell the truth when asked regardless of the consequences. That's what it means to be grown up."

"I'm afraid, Daddy." The catch in her voice slayed him.

A lump formed in his throat. Keaton had to compress his lips between his teeth to bite back a curse. Trying to remain calm, he took several deep breaths.

"What are you afraid of?"

"She'll hit me again."

He closed his eyes. *There it was.* He knew the truth when he heard it. Black rage boiled in his veins. How long had Diane been abusing his daughter, and how the hell had he not known?

It took superhuman effort to remain calm and reassuring when what he really wanted was to hunt Diane down and kill her. "Wait here, baby. I need to get Uncle Coop, okay?"

"Okay."

Keaton strode to the pool deck and let loose a whistle. Both Coop and Knox waved from where they stood talking by the barn. He gestured them to come. As they headed toward the house, he returned to the kitchen and set his phone on the counter for her to play a game.

"Give me one more second, sweetheart." He patted her knee and went back outside to catch Coop before he entered the house.

"What's going on, man?"

"I think Diane's been abusing Chloe, C.C. I need you to help me figure out the truth." A crackle of energy rippled through the air. "What the hell was that?" Keaton asked.

Knox scrubbed his hands over his face. "Sorry. Abuse is my trigger."

Keaton never knew the details of why their cousin came to live with them when he was younger, but he'd long suspected Knox hadn't had a happy start to life. He was too quiet and controlled. "I'm sorry, Knox," he said in a low voice. "I didn't know."

"How could you?" Knox shrugged off the topic with a bitter smile. "The past is the past. Let's figure out what's going on with Chloe."

"How do we go about this? C.C., you're the Sheriff. Is there some sort of protocol?"

"Let's talk to her first. What she views as punishment could vary from what an adult thinks."

The three men entered the kitchen, and Keaton experienced another pang.

Chloe looked small and fragile seated there on the counter. Her legs swung back and forth in her nervousness. But his little girl was made of tougher stuff.

"Hey, midget," Coop said by way of greeting. "I have a few questions for you. Are you up to answering them?"

"Will my mom get in trouble?" Fear caused her voice to crack.

"Here's the thing, midge; if your mom has hurt you, she needs to get help, and you need to be taken away from her care until she does."

Fat teardrops spilled over her lids and tracked down her pale cheeks. "I don't want to get anyone in trouble."

"Well, we have a problem here, midge, because I can't let you go back to a house where I think you might be getting smacked around."

Coop's hard tone triggered Keaton's protective instinct. He'd only taken one step forward before Knox blocked his path.

"Keaton, wait," he urged in a low, quiet tone. "He knows what he's doing."

Coop shot him a warning glance. "I'm talking to you as the Sheriff now, Chloe. I'm going to ask you some questions and record your answers. Do you understand?"

She nodded, and her lower lip trembled where it stuck out.

"Good. Do you want your dad to stay in the room?"

She nodded again.

"Okay. Let's begin…" Coop pulled out his phone and set it to record.

It only took ten minutes to determine Diane had indeed gone beyond the bounds of standard punishments when displeased with Chloe or her behavior.

The bruises on Chloe's arms and legs were not from playing as Keaton had been told time and again. Nausea churned in Keaton's stomach as he'd listened to his daughter relay multiple instances of abuse. Self-disgust was an ugly thing. He'd been a blind fool to miss the signs.

Yes, Diane wasn't the warmest of mothers, and she complained every chance she could, but her vicious actions against his child made him want to kill.

The men left Chloe with a snack and gathered on the deck, making sure they were out of her hearing range.

"I'll need to call Child Services and file a report, Keaton."

"What does that mean for Chloe? Is there the slightest possibility they could take and put her in foster care until they realize it's safe for her to be here? I can't allow that, C.C. She's my daughter. Not to mention she's a young witch coming into her powers," Keaton argued.

"Until this blows over, you could bind her powers like our parents did."

"No! Absolutely not. You see how well that worked out for us." He ran a shaky hand through his hair. "Besides, we didn't know. Chloe does. You think she won't be upset we didn't trust her?"

"We need to bring Zane in on this," Knox said. "As a lawyer, he might have a better solution. He might also be able to file for full custody and get an emergency hearing on Monday."

Keaton grabbed Knox's head between his hands and laid a big smacking kiss on him.

"Dude! What the fuck?"

"That's for being a brilliant motherfucker!"

Coop pulled out his cell phone. "Do it again. I want a picture for his Instagram."

"Fuck you both!" Knox growled good-naturedly.

Keaton slapped Knox on the back. "You only get one chance. You don't know what you're missing."

"Yeah, I'm real broken up about it. Go pedal that crap with Autumn, why don't ya."

"Shit! Autumn! She's supposed to take Chloe for a pedicure."

As if on cue, a vehicle pulled into the drive.

The men peered around the corner of the house as the laughing Thorne sisters piled out of Winnie's SUV.

Autumn was the first to see them and waved. "Is Chloe ready?"

Keaton shook his head. "About that…"

"You don't want her around me." Her voice and expression remained bland, but a deeper study showed her eyes reflected hurt.

"No! That's not it at all." He filled the sisters in on the events of the afternoon and Chloe's confession.

Autumn's white-faced rage mirrored his initial reaction. As she paced, her hands opened and closed in anger.

He approached her cautiously. "Autumn?"

She punched him in the stomach—*hard.*

With the wind knocked out of him, Keaton doubled over.

"Dude!" Knox crowed and stopped Coop from rushing forward. "That is a helluva right."

"Shut up, you asshat!" she raged.

Knox made a sign of zipping his lip and rested his shoulder against the column to watch the show.

She bent over and got in Keaton's face. "You had to pick up that two-bit ho-bag to sleep with and marry, didn't you? Now she's taking out her bitterness and hatred of *you* on your kid. A *great* fucking kid who I would've... would've..." Unable to finish, she shot a vicious kick toward one of the pool lounge chairs. "Fucking dammit!"

When he had his breath back, Keaton straightened. "Are you done?" he asked coldly. He'd had it with violent women.

"No, I'm not done. I won't be done until that bitch is tarred and feathered with her head on a pike in the square." Fury rolled off her in waves.

His anger at Autumn dissolved as suddenly as it had formed. He realized her rage wasn't directed at him. She was furious at the situation—and at Diane in particular. It hadn't gone unnoticed that Autumn had acted more like a mother to his daughter in one week than Diane had in the eight years of Chloe's life.

"Babe." He placed his hands lightly on her shoulders and squeezed. "I know."

She spun about and buried her face in his neck. "She's an innocent kid, Keaton. She doesn't deserve Diane as a mother."

She deserves you, he wanted to say but didn't dare. "If you're still willing, I think she could use that girls' day at Dixie's," he said instead. "It will allow us time to speak with Zane and see what we can come up with custody wise."

Autumn drew away and ran shaking fingertips under her damp eyes. "Of course. Whatever you both need."

The realization he still loved her hit him out of the blue and nearly drove him to his knees.

"Keaton?"

Shell-shocked and light-headed he could only stare.

"Are you okay?" Her hand cupped his cheek, and he closed his eyes.

Moisture burned the back of his lids, and he felt like a complete fool as he stood in front of an audience and fought back tears. "Yeah," he said gruffly. "I need a sec."

He squeezed her hand before he strode away.

CHAPTER 9

*T*he sisters were true to their word and treated Chloe like their honorary Witch Club President. She picked the polish color for their pedicures and decided on the toppings for their pizzas. Dixie created virgin daiquiris for Chloe and Winnie while the others indulged with a shot of rum in their drinks.

"Miss Autumn?"

"Just Autumn."

"Autumn?"

"What's cooking in that brain of yours, small fry?"

"Do you love my dad?"

Autumn froze in the process of sipping her drink. With deliberate care, she set the drink on the side table and shifted into a position identical to Chloe's: shoulder and head resting against the leather seat, facing each other.

Not willing to lie, she said, "I don't know what I feel for your dad. We have a lot of old history between us, and it makes my feelings on the subject a bit confused."

"If my mom hadn't had me, would you love him?"

Autumn's mind tried to wrap itself around the child's logic.

When she regained her wits, she reached for Chloe's hand and interlaced their fingers. "*You* are not now, nor have you ever been, the issue. You certainly won't be our future issue. If anything, your dad's love for you makes him more attractive to me."

"I want you to love my dad," she said tearfully. "I want you to be my mom."

"It doesn't work that way, kid." Autumn lifted their joined hands and dropped a kiss on Chloe's knuckles. "But I will always be a friend, a mentor, and a sister wh—uh, club member—to you," she said with a wink. "I'll always look out for your best interests. Will that work?"

"We'll be besties?"

"Pinky swear."

The two of them interlocked their pinky fingers and shook.

"I love you, Autumn."

"I love you, too, kid."

"Aww, isn't this sweet!" The voice was anything *but* sweet and held a sharp, ugly edge.

Chloe's eyes went wild and her lip trembled.

Autumn shifted in her seat to study the woman with her hands on her hips and a dark scowl on her face.

The years had not been kind to Diane Marshall. Where once she'd been a perky blonde cheerleader at their local high school, now bitterness had etched deep lines in the grooves on either side of her mouth. A permanent wrinkle between her brows marked her tendency to frown a lot. Her bleach-blonde hair, while coiffed perfectly, did nothing to enhance her looks. Diane's brown eyes narrowed and her lips thinned as she glared at their group—and Autumn in particular.

"Chloe, you deliberately disobeyed me. Let's go," Diane commanded, tone edged with a threat of punishment.

Anger sizzled along Autumn's nerve endings and created a pounding in her head. She'd either have a damned stroke or send a fireball straight at the mop Diane called a hairdo.

Autumn surged to her feet and waved off the nail technician. "Chloe isn't going anywhere with you, Diane." She directed her next comment over her shoulder without removing her gaze from Chloe's mother. "Summer, call Coop and Keaton. There is about to be an incident."

"You cannot keep me from my daughter. I don't care if you *are* screwing my husband."

Tired of accusations, Autumn raised her index finger. "First, that language is not appropriate in front of a child." She held up a second finger. "Second, last I checked, Keaton isn't your husband. He hasn't been for close to five years." She held up a third finger. "And third, not that it's your business, but no, you effectively destroyed anything he and I might've had years ago. I'm sure you're still patting yourself on the back for that one."

"You're a liar! Everyone knows the Thorne sisters are whores!"

Based on her conversation with her virgin sister earlier today, Autumn found the statement laughable. "Wow! If that isn't the pot calling the kettle black, I don't know what is. But I'm only going to warn you this one last time to watch your mouth in front of Chloe."

"You act like you're such a badass, Autumn. What did you do when Keaton turned to me? Nothing! You ran away like a whiny baby," Diane sneered.

Water sloshed behind Autumn, and Chloe stepped into view with her sparkly purple sneakers clutched to her chest. Dread and fear made the child's face pale.

"Don't yell at her anymore, Mama. I'll go with you."

Chloe's bravery was admirable, but there was no way in hell Autumn would allow her to be alone with Diane again. "No, you absolutely will *not* go with her!" Autumn said as she stepped between mother and daughter. "Chloe, please go back to your chair and finish your pizza. We will continue to enjoy our afternoon when I get back." She grabbed Diane by her flabby upper arm. "Come with me," she ground out.

She wasn't surprised when her nemesis dragged her feet, but

Autumn wasn't a skilled witch for nothing. She mouthed a silent incantation and forced Diane to fall in line.

Autumn didn't stop until she'd propelled Diane to the narrow alleyway beside the old brick building. With one hand to the other woman's throat, she pinned her to the wall.

"Let's get something straight, bitch," she growled. "If you ever lay a hand on that kid again, I'll personally rip it the fuck off."

"This is assault!"

"You haven't seen assault yet, but I promise you, you'll see it up close and personal if you hurt Chloe again."

"She's my child. I'll discipline her the way I see fit," Diane yelled into her face.

Autumn had a difficult time reining in her fury. "Try me. Just fucking *try* me, Diane." She hauled back and slammed the smaller woman into the bricks. Sometimes it helped to be Amazon-sized.

"You think because you're Keaton's flavor-of-the-month that you can get away with treating me like this. I'll see you in jail for attacking me."

"And you think because you're Chloe's mother that you can get away with smacking her around or belittling her?" Autumn's voice rose in relation to her rage. "It doesn't work that way. *Not in this town.* One word to the supposed friends you value so much, and you'll be blackballed. No more invitations to parties or inclusion in what constitutes society events. Poor, lonely little Diane will have no more friends." Autumn sneered her disgust. "Keaton may not tear you a new asshole because you're a woman, but I have no such problem."

"You can't threaten me!"

"I think she just did," a dry voice inserted.

Diane's eyes went wide at the sight of the man entering the alley.

Autumn didn't need to turn to see who had joined their little party. No one's voice contained the arrogance of Alastair Thorne. "Hello, Uncle."

"Toying with the locals again, niece?"

"I have a real issue with child abusers," Autumn returned, never removing her fierce gaze from Diane. "Makes me want to *kill* something."

"You remind me of my dear departed mother. She was as fierce as she was beautiful. Could never tolerate others who put on airs." He strolled casually in their direction as if he had all day. "She especially hated bullies. Why, she had the perfect remedy. But back then people could practically get away with murder."

"Oh, I don't know, Uncle. Something tells me I might get away with murder if I planned it carefully."

His wicked laugh echoed off the stones around them. "Yes, child, I believe you could." When he reached them, he placed a fingertip on the crevice between Diane's brows. "But enough of this. There are more important matters that need your attention." He murmured a smattering of Latin, and Diane's gaze went blank. "You'll never hurt your child again in any way. Go home, have some wine, and think kind thoughts about my lovely niece, Autumn." He snapped his fingers.

Like a mindless zombie, Diane walked in the direction of the parking lot.

"Nice," Autumn muttered. "I need to learn that trick."

"I'll be happy to teach you. *After* you retrieve my stone."

"You're like a damned dog with a bone, you know that?"

She gestured to the retreating Diane. "Will she be able to drive home okay?"

"Do you care?"

She didn't, but she would feel guilty if Diane took out someone else in the process. "I don't want to see anyone else hurt."

"She'll be fine. Consider it autopilot mode."

"I need to get back to Chloe."

"When do you leave for China?"

"How did you know we narrowed the stone's location to China?"

Amusement lit his sapphire eyes. "I have my ways."

Suspicion clouded her mind. "Holly or Quentin? Which one is your little spy?"

Alastair's arrogant air dropped, and for a moment, he seemed as if he cared. "I'm sorry you were hurt to the point you trust no one."

Unexpected emotion clogged her throat, and tears burned her eyes. Her unpredicted response to his empathy had her swallowing hard. "I trust people."

"No, child, you don't. But perhaps it's a good thing."

Autumn dug deep to find her standard sass. "You aren't getting all sentimental and shit, are you? The last thing I need is for you to get all touchy-feely on me."

His delighted laughter echoed throughout the alley. "If I didn't know better, I'd say you were my mother reincarnated. Promise me you'll never change."

The scuffle of soles on pavement behind her indicated someone running in her direction.

"Autumn!" Keaton skidded to a halt next to her. "Where's Diane?"

"She went home."

He glanced between her and Alastair. "In a pine box?"

She bit her lip to hold back an inappropriate giggle. "No. But my uncle wasn't above a little mind control. I believe *if* Diane is ever around Chloe again, she may be a better mother."

Keaton's dark brows rose skyward, and he addressed Alastair. "How long will the mind control last?" Another thought occurred to him, and he frowned in her direction. He lowered his voice to ask, "Isn't doing that against the laws of witchcraft or something?"

"I didn't do it. I don't believe in taking someone's free will," she stressed. If her tone was sharper than normal, it couldn't be helped. She was fed up with the constant insinuation that she was a puppet master to the people around her. "Now, if you'll excuse me, I'll finish my pedicure." She made it five steps when Keaton cut her off.

"Babe, I didn't mean it like that." He placed his right hand over his heart. "I swear to you, here and now, that I truly believe I love —*loved*—you of my own free will."

"You're not still angry I bound you from speaking the truth?"

"Maybe a little. But I think I'm more disgusted with myself because I didn't give you a choice."

"It's like you kids have made up. We should have a celebration," snarked Alastair.

"Way to kill a moment, old man."

Alastair's droll mood turned deadly. "Mind your tongue, boy. I don't particularly care for your tone."

The frigid quality of Alastair's voice unnerved Autumn. She rushed to intercede. "I leave the day after tomorrow for China. I should have a bead on the stone's location by the day after at the latest."

Her uncle nodded, cast one last long look at Keaton, and teleported away.

"I am never going to get used to people disappearing into thin air," Keaton said as he raised a hand to run through his already mussed hair.

"You will. It will be second nature to you soon enough," she assured him. "Come on, let's see about Chloe. I'm afraid Diane was as ugly as she could be, and your kid had a first-hand view of the drama." Autumn filled him in on the details of the confrontation as they walked toward the salon.

When she finished, he backed her up against the wall and rested both hands on either side of her head. "Thank you for protecting my little girl," he said gruffly. "I owe you more than words can say."

Because his intensity made her uneasy, she concentrated on the passing gawkers. "We should get back," she hedged.

"Babe."

Inch by inch she turned her head to face him, unable to ignore the emotion he projected in that one word.

Words were unnecessary. They always had been. The feelings between Autumn and Keaton transcended the ordinary. One look, one touch, one kiss said it all.

He lowered his head and brushed his lips softly against hers. Once, twice, and at the third contact, he slipped his tongue between her parted lips. Time stood still as Autumn drank in his desire. Whatever fire had burned ten years ago was nothing compared to what she experienced today.

She loved him. The simple realization struck her right there on main street. With nothing but his mouth on hers and a husky "thank you," he'd laid waste to all her carefully erected walls.

CHAPTER 10

*C*hloe, who'd been hovering by the front window of the salon, flew into Autumn's embrace the moment the front door opened.

"Hey! It's okay, kid," she said, hugging the child tight.

"Can I stay?"

"Pfft. Of course! No one is taking our club president away." Autumn lifted Chloe in a fireman hold and skipped to the pedicure station. The little girl laughed her delight.

The sight melted Keaton's heart. This was how a mother and child should be together. He followed the two loves of his life through the salon.

"Can I, Dad?" Chloe asked from where she now perched on her pedicure throne. The faux purple stones in her tiara caught the light as she lifted her pleading eyes to him.

"Can you what?"

"Can I get a facial?"

"I'm not sure it's…" Seeing the disappointment start to cloud her features, he changed his tune. "Sure."

Autumn bit her lip to curb her amused grin. She cleared her throat, and he suspected it was to hide the laughter bubbling up. "It's a mini-facial and will take about a half hour. If it's all right with you, we want to turn this into a spa day."

"Is it girls only?" he asked.

"You want to get your toes painted, Keaton?" she taunted.

He eyed the tub of water containing her feet. "I don't know about the polish, but soaking my feet would be nice."

"Here, Daddy. Take my spot. Miss Dixie is finished with mine."

Keaton tweaked Chloe's nose before lifting her, settling into the chair, and setting her on his lap. "Don't mind if I do." He took a large bite of his daughter's leftover pizza and grinned at Autumn while he chewed.

"This was supposed to be a girls' day," Autumn said archly.

He glanced around at the other Thorne women in the salon. None of them seemed to be bothered he was here. As a matter of fact, Winnie shot him a wink that he took for encouragement.

"Should we put it to a vote?" Spring asked laughingly. "All in favor of Keaton joining our party, say aye."

Four of the five said aye. The only one left to vote was Autumn, and he faced her with a raised brow. "Is this majority rules or does it have to be unanimous?"

"Majority rules," Winnie piped up. "Tums's vote doesn't count."

"Still, I don't want to stay where I'm not wanted," he told her.

"You're wanted," Autumn replied softly. So low that he almost missed it.

His heart picked up its pace and did its best impression of a jack-hammer. The underlying meaning of her words was not lost.

"But to be a true member, you have to have your toes polished," she added with a flash of her dimple followed by a mischievous chuckle.

"I'll have you know, I am not afraid to pocket my man-card for the day and have my toenails polished. Chloe went through a purple polish stage about two years ago. I fell victim to her pleading."

The women all laughed.

"Daiquiri or beer?" Summer asked.

"Whatever the rest of the party is having," he returned.

"Daiquiri it is."

Within minutes he was drinking the best strawberry-flavored froufrou drink he'd ever had. "I think men don't realize what they're missing," he said with a contented sigh as the warm water bubbled around his feet and ankles.

The rest of the afternoon was spent in a swirl of activity. Manicures, facials, hair styles. When they were all finished, Chloe lingered by the makeup display, a look of longing on her face.

He started forward, only to be stopped by a hand on his arm.

"Can I treat her to a lip gloss?" Autumn asked, careful to keep her voice low. "I know some parents feel eight is young, but I think she only wants to bond with another female."

"Does it show that I'm lost at sea here?" he asked with a self-conscious laugh.

"It shows you are a caring father, Keaton. She's lucky to have you."

He loved Autumn more in that moment than he ever had. She understood his struggle and didn't mock him.

"She can have whatever she wants."

"Okay, *some* restraint on your part wouldn't be remiss," she laughed.

"Would it be better if I leave the whole thing in your hands?"

"Possibly."

He waved a hand toward Chloe. "Be my guest."

"Watch and learn," Autumn sassed.

Oh, he had no problem watching. He could watch her walk away all day with a curvy ass like hers.

As if she felt his gaze locked on her lush ass, she cast a last look over her shoulder.

He winked.

Her fiery blush pleased him. She could deny their connection all she wanted, but whatever they shared hadn't been completely lost. He had hope that he could build on what remained of her feelings for him.

For the next few minutes, he observed Autumn teach the fine art of makeup application to his daughter. Any other father would be dying inside at the idea of his little girl trying to be older, but Chloe needed the bonding time with another female.

"She's good with her, isn't she?" Winnie said from beside him.

"She is. Chloe missed that type of attention growing up."

"Autumn was never the monster you painted her, Keaton," she said with a hint of censure.

"I know." He faced her and allowed her to see his honest, raw emotions. "I was a fool. My only excuse was fear. Plain and simple."

"Why did you sleep with Diane that night? To punish my sister?"

"God, no!" He hadn't realized he'd practically shouted his response until the occupants of the salon turned toward him. He lowered his voice for Winnie's ears alone. "Until Autumn walked in and woke me—er, us—I had no idea I'd even had sex with Diane. I was trashed that night, Winnie. I still don't remember the act itself." He screwed up his mouth in self-disgust. "A friend of mine said that Diane came onto me. Like I said, I don't remember."

The whole incident left a bitter taste in his mouth.

"Why did you never seek Autumn out to explain?" she asked quietly.

"A number of reasons. Part of me was still angry with her for what she'd withheld. I was also embarrassed by my reaction. Then there was the irrational belief that my feelings for her weren't my own." He sighed and shook his head. "But mostly, what I did was unforgivable."

"Not unforgivable. I think a part of her has already forgiven you." Winnie smiled. "I mean, she *has* started talking to you again and hasn't threatened to turn you into a toadstool in at least a week."

"Thank God for small favors," he muttered.

"Goddess," Winnie corrected with a laugh. "You are officially pagan now, Mr. Warlock."

"I've known about magic for nearly ten years and still can't wrap my head around it."

"True, but you didn't live it every day." She patted his arm before walking away.

Winnie was wrong. He *had* lived with it every day. There hadn't been one single day that went by since his breakup with Autumn when he didn't relive their fight. Sometimes he'd been angry when recalling the events, and sometimes he'd been sad. But he'd thought of Autumn constantly.

"OKAY, HERE'S THE THING; WE WANT TO CONTINUE OUR LITTLE HEN party at the house," Autumn told Keaton. "Disney flicks, popcorn, and slumber party."

"I'm in."

The sexy way he growled the words, for her ears alone, caused her nether region to tingle. She tried to remind herself they'd never had a problem when it came to sex, but risking her heart to him again was foolish on every level.

Her brows lifted, and she slapped her let's-get-real face firmly in place. "*You* are not invited. Last time I checked, and forgive me because it's been a while, you weren't a hen. You were more of the rooster variety."

He grinned, and the wickedness of it stole her breath.

"No," she said, applying the word to all things sexual in nature.

"Oh, I don't know. I'm pretty good at arranging hair and talking about… things. Should we put it to another vote?"

His words brought to mind the times he would run his fingers through Autumn's hair after they'd made love. They would lay about as he removed the tangles and talk about everything and nothing. No subject had been off limits, and they'd had the most interesting debates. Ones that usually ended in a rousing bout of lovemaking.

Because she needed space from her memories, she said, "I'm overruling everyone."

"But you aren't the WC president," he taunted. "That's Chloe's position. I think she'll do her old dad a solid."

"Let me put this another way. If you join us tonight, I'm not having dinner with you tomorrow."

"Ah, babe, you drive a hard bargain. Do you need me to drop anything by for her tonight? PJs or a toothbrush?"

"We can conjure anything she needs," Autumn assured him.

"She has a special bear she likes to sleep with."

"You're determined to come by, aren't you?"

"Other than her staying with her mom, it's her first sleep-over," he admitted, sheepishness written all over his expression.

Dammit! Didn't he look adorable in his concern for his daughter?

"How about I get your number and text you when she's ready for bed? You can bring her bear and tuck her in."

"Thank you," he said, his tone low and intimate.

"Off with you." Or the walls of ice around her heart would melt to mere puddles of water.

He studied her for a short while, and his eyes seemed a little lighter, perhaps a bit brighter. "You are one in a million, Autumn Thorne," he said. The husky timbre of his voice curled inside her and made her long for things she shouldn't want.

To hide her thoughts, she whipped out her cell. "What's your number?"

He rattled off seven digits then brushed past her to scoop his daughter into a hug. "Be good for Autumn, okay?"

"Yes, Daddy."

"I'll see you tonight when I drop off your things. I love you, Chloe."

Autumn's stomach flipped at his words. She hadn't heard them spoken from him in what felt like forever. Granted they weren't directed at her, but with those three little words, he brought her back to the first time he'd uttered them to her.

They'd gone skiing, just the two of them. But a terrible snow storm had rolled in that day, and because the ski patrol advised against going up the mountain, the two of them had stayed tucked away in their tiny chalet. They'd been snuggled together in front of the large stone hearth, wrapped around each other under a blanket as they sipped wine.

"I love you, Autumn." Keaton had said the words without any fanfare or warning. A simple statement.

She twisted around to see his expression. What she saw was a man who stood behind the conviction of his words.

"I love you too, Keaton."

That night, there was a new element to their lovemaking. They took their time making love, as if they had all the time in the world. They worshipped each other's bodies with each kiss and every caress, letting their bodies speak for them.

Keaton had told her at least ten more times within the next twenty-four hours. And until the day she'd walked into his bedroom and saw him in bed with her best friend, she never doubted his affection.

"Are you all right?"

Keaton's concerned voice brought her back from the past in a rush.

"Yes."

The false smile fooled no one. He would've commented, but Chloe spoke up at that precise instant, diverting his attention.

Autumn breathed a sigh of relief. She wouldn't lie, but she didn't want to rehash the past. Nothing good would come of going down that road. She needed to find a way to cancel tomorrow's date. Perhaps she needed to rethink his assistance in China too. Keaton had the potential to lay waste to her carefully reconstructed world.

CHAPTER 11

*L*ater that evening, Keaton swung by to drop off Chloe's bear and tuck her in as promised. He noticed the sisters had conjured a perfect little girl's room for his daughter, filled with purple butterflies and all things magical. Autumn's old room held no trace of the past. He experienced a pang in the region of his heart for what once was.

When he walked downstairs, Autumn and two of her sisters were gathered in the living room, sipping wine. They wore cute footie pajamas to match Chloe's set. As one, they looked up as he entered the room.

His eyes zeroed in on Autumn, as they always did. "Thanks for being kind to Chloe. She'd had a rough go of it."

"You don't have to thank me, Keaton. I truly adore her." She nodded to Winnie and Spring. "We all do."

"Still, she's lonely and…" He broke off, unable to voice the pain he felt on his daughter's behalf.

"Would you like a glass of wine?" Spring asked him kindly.

"I'd love one."

"Red or white?"

"Whatever is open will be fine," he assured her with a smile.

She rose and gestured to her spot next to Autumn. "Take a load off. You've had a rough day too."

Keaton's eyes sought Autumn's for permission. Although wary, she nodded and shifted to make room on the couch for his larger frame.

"Cute PJs," he said.

"Winnie's idea when Chloe said what she wanted hers to look like."

At a loss for words, he stared.

When she ducked her head, he drew back the heavy curtain of auburn hair from her face and tucked it behind her ear.

She cleared her throat and looked anywhere but at him. "I don't think dinner tomorrow is a good idea," she blurted.

"In general, or with me?" He'd suspected she would try to wheedle out of the date once she had a chance to think about it.

Winnie popped up. "Would you look at the time! I have to check internet orders."

"Not subtle at all, sister," Autumn snarked.

Winnie grinned. "Can't say I didn't try to make it seem legit."

Keaton would've laughed had he not been pissed that Autumn was trying to cancel on him.

Spring returned with a glass of red wine and followed Winnie from the room.

Left alone, Autumn had no choice but to face him.

"With you," she said, answering his earlier question. "We aren't who we used to be. Too much water has flowed under that bridge, Keaton."

"Here's the thing: whatever we had, it's not dead." He lifted her hand and placed it flat over his heart. "Feel that? It happens whenever I see you walk into a room. Whenever you're near, my heart goes into overdrive. I don't care if I live to be one hundred. It's never going away."

She remained silent.

"I think you feel it, too." He laid his palm flat over her heart. "I'm sure of it."

"Thornes only love once. But that doesn't mean I can ever trust you again," she said not unkindly. There was no malice in her words, just honest fear to believe in him again.

"I love you. I always have, and I always will." He pushed past the apprehension building inside.

"But your kind of love isn't what I want. I need someone stronger than you'll ever be."

He stopped breathing. When he started again, his lungs felt heavy, as if he inhaled lungfuls of water and was on the verge of drowning.

"Stronger?" he had the presence of mind to ask.

"Someone who won't run into another woman's arms the second we've argued or after they've become blindingly drunk."

"I was a stupid kid, Autumn." His head fell back against the cushions. "How can I prove to you it will never happen again?"

"I don't know that you can. But you have to understand what seeing the two of you together did to me, Keaton. It broke me." She took a ragged breath. "You not only rejected all that I was—*am*—in that clearing, you turned to someone else within hours."

No words could defend his actions. Hell, more than anyone, he knew how indefensible they were.

"When I opened your door, when I saw you in bed together—the man I loved and my best friend—I died. Or the Autumn I was back then did. At least in part. Then the baby..." She shook her head. "I'm still dead inside. There are moments when warmth seeps in, like spending time with Chloe and my sisters, but otherwise I feel nothing."

"Christ, Autumn! I'm so sorry."

"I know you are. I am, too. But it changes nothing." She took a sip of wine while she stared at the low-burning flames of the fire-place. "We can't go back and undo the past. But perhaps we can go forward as friends."

"I'm not sure I can handle only being your friend."

Finally, she turned her face toward his. "It's easier than the enemies we've been until now, don't you think?"

"I don't know. At least when I despised you, I felt it was justified. In a weird way, it kept me going."

"I know what you mean. I think we lived to taunt one another."

He laughed, but it sounded hollow even to his own ears.

"I don't want to hate you, Keaton. But I can't love you either."

"Where does that leave us?"

"Right where we are. I will train you, Coop, and Chloe until I feel you are ready to be on your own. Then I go home to Maine for good."

"In the meantime, there's a magical stone to find," he reminded her.

"Yes, there is that. I understand if you don't want to go with me. Maybe it would be better if you didn't."

"I'm going. It's the least I can do for you."

She cupped his jaw. "You don't have to try to make up for anything. You know that, right?"

He turned his head and placed a light kiss in the center of her palm. "And yet, I do."

Frustration and something resembling resignation settled over her features. "Fair enough." She rose and set her glass of wine on the coffee table. "I'll see you out."

"You should give that poor boy a second chance."

The warm voice startled Autumn from the trance she'd been in since Keaton drove away. And because she knew to whom the voice belonged, she didn't bother to turn around. "It isn't that easy, Aunt GiGi."

"Why?"

"He can't be trusted."

"He's suffered as much as you, child."

Temper rising, Autumn spun her upper body to face GiGi. "Has he? It wasn't him who walked in on me screwing his best friend. It wasn't him who carried a child for four months only to lose it, and with it, any ability to bear another." She struggled to regain control. "Please, don't tell me how much he's suffered. In my opinion, it wasn't enough."

And maybe that was what was bothering Autumn. Perhaps deep inside, she didn't feel it was fair to let him off scot-free.

"So that is what this is? It's about making him suffer more in order for his pain to be equal to yours?" GiGi asked coolly.

"I'm a grown-ass woman, Aunt GiGi. I don't need your attempts to manipulate me," Autumn said, warning evident in her tone.

In truth, she didn't want to play any of this over again in her mind. She was tired of the back and forth. But it also seemed wrong to have GiGi stick up for Keaton. Who had ever stuck up for her in all this? Everyone's subtle maneuvering to throw Autumn and Keaton together irritated her.

GiGi stepped in close and towered over her. "You are stuck in the past."

"*I* am? That's rich, coming from you."

"Just what are you implying?"

"I know, better than most, that Thornes only love once. But did that have to stop you from moving on? From going after your husband to iron things out? And barring that, perhaps have a lover or two to while away the long nights?"

Before Autumn's eyes, her aunt's complexion paled, and she took on a devastated, haunted look.

Shit! Taking her hurt and anger out on her aunt wasn't cool. "I'm sorry. You didn't deserve my ugly."

"I do love my husband, Autumn. It's the reason I haven't 'moved on'. Not too different from you, I imagine."

The frosty tone and the raised chin spoke of GiGi's wounded pride. Autumn couldn't blame her aunt for the bite in her words. Hitting below the belt was uncalled for.

"I really am sorry. I know you love Uncle Ryker."

No one could really say what went down between GiGi and Ryker other than the fact their fights used to be epic battles. But

Autumn supposed the fire between two such passionate individuals had to eventually die out.

"Yes, well, Ryker isn't the issue here. You and Keaton are."

"Just as you don't care to discuss your relationship woes, I don't want to discuss mine." Autumn stood and dusted off the seat of her pajama bottoms. She took a sniff of the air. "Do I smell brownies?"

"You do, but I don't know if ungrateful nieces should be allowed any of my award-winning delights."

"You're a cruel woman, Aunt GiGi."

"And don't you forget it." A second or two passed before GiGi softened. "Now come. Let's eat brownies and drown our sorrows."

"I suspect you are trying to soften me up for one of your lectures."

"That, too."

As they took their seats around the kitchen table—the go-to discussion spot for all things family related—GiGi served up an extra-large square of the tasty treat.

As she sank her teeth into the chocolatey goodness, Autumn moaned her pleasure.

"Rumor has it you are going after the Chintamani Stone for Alastair," GiGi said casually.

Autumn choked on the brownie. She and her sisters hadn't purposely kept the information from GiGi, but neither had they gone out of their way to tell her. None of them wanted the argument that would ensue if their aunt knew they were helping Alastair.

When she could draw air into her lungs without coughing, she said, "I'm not going after the stone. I'm going on a recon mission."

"For Alastair," GiGi said darkly.

"For my mother," Autumn countered.

"You should leave them both to their fate." The sourness in her aunt's tone couldn't be missed.

"What did my mother ever do to you?"

"She left you kids to fend for yourselves."

"We were young, but we weren't babies, Aunt GiGi. You and Dad took care of us well enough."

An unnamed emotion flashed in the other woman's eyes before she could look away.

Autumn set the brownie in the center of her plate and took care in forming her next questions. "Were we that much of an obligation? Is that why Uncle Ryker left?"

"Ryker left for his own reasons, and you girls mean the world to me."

GiGi's evasiveness didn't go unnoticed. Something deeper was at play here, but Autumn was damned if she could figure it out.

"If there is a chance to help my mother, I'm going to take it," she said softly. "It's not meant to hurt you. Please know that."

With a clearing of her throat, GiGi stood and patted Autumn's shoulder. "It's getting late, dear. We'll talk again soon. But in the meantime, don't be so hard on Keaton. People change."

After GiGi exited the kitchen, Autumn was left to wonder what the hell tonight's visit was all about. It seemed her aunt's mission was two-fold; find out what Autumn knew about Alastair's plans for the stone and convince her to make up with Keaton.

Autumn sighed and rose to her feet. A muffled sound had her spinning around.

"Chloe! You startled me. Are you okay?"

The girl nodded her dark head.

"Was it scary to wake up in a strange house?" Autumn asked gently.

Again, Chloe nodded.

She opened her arms to the child. "Come here."

Chloe ran to her and cuddled into her embrace. "I was scared," the girl admitted.

"I can understand that. Do you want me to take you home?"

"Will you be mad at me for not staying?"

"Of course not, sweetie. This was your day. If you want to go home, then that's what we'll do."

A minute passed before Chloe spoke. "Why did that woman say you were hard on my dad?"

Autumn searched her brain for an answer. How the hell was she supposed to explain her relationship to a kid?

"A long time ago, your dad and I dated. We had a misunderstanding, and I'm finding it difficult to separate then and now. Do you understand?"

"I think so," Chloe said. "At school, Mary Beth pushed me down on the playground and laughed at me. Then she wanted to be my friend."

"What did you tell her?"

"That I didn't want her to be my friend because she was mean."

"Is she still being mean to you?"

"Not really. I think she's sad."

"Sounds like you do understand. We seem to have the same problem." Autumn touched a fingertip to Chloe's cute, upturned nose. "Come on. You go gather your things, and I'll wrap up a couple of brownies for you and your dad."

The sunny smile rewarded her offer of sweets.

Within ten minutes, Autumn had pulled up to the Carlyle estate. The lights were on, indicating the occupants of the house were still awake.

"Ready?" she asked Chloe.

"Ready."

Hand-in-hand, they approached the house. Keaton must've heard the car doors close because he met them on the porch.

"Hey! What's this?"

Chloe ran into his outstretched arms, and Autumn had a moment of envy.

"She woke up in a strange place, and it scared her a bit," she explained.

Keaton kissed the top of Chloe's dark head and squatted in front of her. "That happened to me as a kid, too."

"I'm sorry, Daddy."

"What's to be sorry about? I don't mind you wanting to come home."

Chloe flung her arms around his neck, and Autumn had a sense of how much Diane's horrific behavior affected the poor girl. Chloe was afraid to upset the adults in her life.

Autumn held up the paper bag in her hand. "Don't forget your brownies, kid."

"Brownies?" Keaton picked up Chloe and balanced her on his shoulders. "This is the first I'm hearing about brownies. Were you holding out on me, midget?"

The child's happy giggle eased Autumn's own tension. She approached and handed Keaton the bag. Their eyes connected, and she had the insane urge to kiss him. Not a sexual take-me-now-big-boy type of kiss, but a quick peck on the mouth that spoke of affection.

His eyes crinkled as he smiled. She noticed the bold laugh lines bracketing his mouth. Somehow, the small sign of aging made him more attractive.

"Thanks for thinking of me, babe."

Her toes curled in her shoes. The husky timbre of his voice did odd things to her insides. "My pleasure."

The smile lines deepened further with his laugh, and she knew, without him ever having to voice his thoughts, what he was thinking.

"I, uh, I gotta go," she mumbled. Autumn got three feet before she remembered his daughter. She spun around but continued to walk backward. "Thanks for a lovely day, Chloe. I had fun."

"Me, too, Miss Autumn."

"Just Autumn," she reminded her. "I'll see you tomorrow for training."

"Good night, babe." Keaton's voice wrapped around her and caused an involuntary shudder of delight.

"Good night, Keaton."

CHAPTER 12

*T*wo days later, Autumn, Summer, Coop, and Keaton sat on the floor of the attic, discussing the China trip.

"Since I've seen pictures of the monastery, I can teleport us to the exterior of the building," Autumn said. "The problem comes with gaining entry. Will they just let us through the front door if we show up?"

"It's a monastery. Aren't they supposed to be Zen and shit? Why would they turn you away?" Coop asked.

"That's the question of the hour," Keaton muttered. "I guess we take our chances. Is there any indication where the stone might be or what it's disguised as? I can't imagine they are simply going to hand it over. Does that mean stealing it? If so, what happens if we get caught?"

"From what research I could gather, the stone was set in some godawful necklace design. Trust me, you'll know it when you see it. But here, I've sketched it." Summer laid a piece of paper in the center of the group. "And in reference to stealing, don't get caught."

"What is with this family and breaking the law?" Coop muttered.

"If it's any consolation, my love, any broken laws will be on foreign soil and out of your jurisdiction," Summer laughed and kissed his cheek. "You're a warlock now. You'll have to get used to lying and bending the law to hide what you are."

Coop graced the group with a sour look. "I need to get back to work. Stay out of trouble." He turned to his brother. "Stay safe and don't do anything reckless. The one person with enough magic to bail you out will be with you. And based on your past history, I'm guessing she'll leave your ass behind."

Autumn let loose a wicked laugh when Keaton cast her a wary glance. If she had to guess, he was beginning to realize the stupidity of putting himself at her mercy. If he still planned on accompanying her, he'd grown nads the size of bowling balls.

Keaton studied her for another minute then smiled. "Nah. She wouldn't dare. If she did, she'd be forced to explain to Chloe, and I suspect she'd find that hard to do because she adores my kid."

Damn, the man had her figured out. Not good. "True. For Chloe's sake, I'd save your ass."

"That works for me," he laughed. "When do we leave?"

Autumn stood and held out a hand to haul her sister to her feet. "There's an eleven-hour difference between here and there. I'd like to arrive tomorrow morning, which means we leave here tonight around nine. That puts us there about eight a.m."

"Perfect. That gives me time to tuck Chloe in. I'll be here at eight-thirty tonight." Keaton rose in one smooth motion. "Shoot me a text with what I'll need."

The sisters shared an amused look.

"What?" he asked as he moved a little too close for Autumn's comfort.

"We travel light and conjure what we need when we get to where we're going," she explained and edged away.

"Gotcha." With a warm smile for Summer, he asked, "Do you mind giving me a minute alone with Autumn?"

Nerves ate at the lining of Autumn's stomach. What did they possibly have to discuss in private? She nearly grabbed for Summer's arm as her sister nodded and headed out after Coop.

"How's this going to work if you can't stand to look at me or touch me, babe?"

He had a point. Since the other night, she'd found it difficult to be around him. With her anger gone, she had no protective barrier against him. "I don't know. For over nine years, we've been at odds. I'm not sure how to be me around you. But it would help if you cut out the pet names."

Keaton steepled his hands over his mouth before he rubbed his eyes. "Sorry. Being around you again…it's brought back all the good memories, too, ya know?"

Unexpected tears burned her eyes. She *did* know. For the length of time their relationship had lasted, it had been beautiful. Every day better than the last. In hindsight, it couldn't possibly have remained that way. The first bloom of love was bound to rub off, and then where would they have been?

"Hey," he said softly and cradled her face in his palms. "What's this?"

"I don't know. The more I spend time with you, the more I find odd, stray emotions creep up and attack me from behind."

He drew her into his embrace and rested his cheek against her temple. She loved how feminine he made her feel with the simple gesture.

"You aren't alone in your feelings, Autumn. But mixed in there, I have a lot of self-hatred, sorrow, and regret." He sighed and kissed her forehead. "Had I been the slightest bit open and understanding about your gifts, we wouldn't be at this point in our lives."

"It couldn't have lasted, Keaton. Nothing good ever does," she said in a low, aching voice.

"Not true. Some people make it work. Look at Coop's dispatcher, Lil. She's been married to the same man for nearly forty years." He drew back and bent a little to meet her downcast gaze. "And the Johnsons. They are celebrating their sixtieth anniversary next month. Things last. But they take a mutual respect and willingness to work at it."

Autumn met his intense gaze and got lost there. When he inched his mouth toward hers, she didn't protest. And when his lips hovered over hers, she rose on her toes to close the distance between them.

This kiss was like no other. Their standard level of passion was present, but this had the added qualities of age and wisdom. This kiss redefined how kissing should be. It contained love and appreciation for stolen moments. It hinted at a desperation due to an unclear future, but contained hope all the same.

As her hands wound into Keaton's dark hair, Autumn played with its thick, smooth texture. His arms came more fully around her and pulled her close. The ridge of his budding erection rubbed against her abdomen, and she wanted to purr like a contented kitten at its feel.

They broke off with tiny lingering kisses and love bites. Keaton pressed his pelvis into her once before backing off. It was as if the gesture was more instinctual in nature and his brain had to override his body's command.

"I'd better go. If I don't, I'm going to beg you for sexual favors." His voice was deep and throaty. It reached in and caressed her.

Goddess, she wanted to throw caution to the winds and drag him to the nearest bed, but her baser urges would get her in trouble. More and more often, she had to remind herself that he was untrustworthy. That he could destroy her this time around if she wasn't careful.

Because breaking contact was difficult, she finger-combed his rumpled hair and ran a hand down his shirt to smooth the wrinkles. "I'll see you tonight."

"Don't say it in that voice, or I don't care how much you resist, I'll sweep you up and drag you to my private lair," he warned.

The visual gave her a warm shiver of appreciation.

After a mental slap, she said, "Go."

"My biggest regret was my stupid-ass reaction in the clearing." He toyed with a shoulder seam on her top, and if Autumn didn't know better, she'd have sworn he was nervous. "If I had it to do over, I can't say that I wouldn't do the same thing—but only because of my daughter. I would never want to erase her from my life."

"I understand that, Keaton."

His tortured gaze lifted to hers. "What you don't understand is how much I wish she was yours. Ours."

Tears flooded her eyes. Her nose and throat burned with the effort to hold back the sobs that wanted to break loose. "Oh, Keaton."

He rested his forehead against hers. "You don't have to answer me now. But think about us and about giving me a second chance. I probably don't deserve one, yet I want one so badly I..." He cleared his throat. "Just think about it."

Keaton didn't seem to expect an answer, which was good because Autumn didn't trust herself to speak.

They shared one more tight hug then he left her alone in the attic.

"ARE YOU READY?" AUTUMN ASKED LATER THAT EVENING.

Keaton didn't want to admit he was apprehensive about teleporting. He'd seen the Thornes pop in and out with barely a snap of their fingers. But for someone who had never teleported to another room, traveling to another continent was scary as hell.

As if she guessed his reservations, she said, "We can do a few trial runs. I can transport you to the barn or outside to get you used to it."

"Won't that drain you for the real thing?"

She laughed and shook her head. "No. Magic isn't draining. Or that use isn't."

"I'm assuming it doesn't scramble your organs or anything like in a bad sci-fi movie."

"Promise."

He wiped his sweaty palms on his jeans. "What do we need for clothing and essentials? You said I didn't need to pack."

"I can conjure anything we need if we are there that long," she assured him. "But we do need heavy coats, lined pants, and sturdy weather-proof boots. I'm teleporting us to a general location. We'll probably need to hike a ways."

"Can I conjure, or am I still too much of a novice?"

"You want to learn now? We have a little time to spare."

He nodded his agreement.

"Okay, let's try something small like a piece of fruit," she suggested and held out her hand, palm up. "In your mind, visualize an apple. I'd go with your favorite type."

Keaton closed his eyes and formed the apple in his mind. "Okay."

"Good. Now, think of the apple's composition. The skin, the fleshy interior, the core, and the seeds. Can you see it?"

"Yes."

"Good. Next, fire up the magic inside you like when you lifted the water from the bowl. Then, imagine the weight of the apple in your hand," she instructed.

He did as she commanded, and when his fingers closed around a solid, round object, he opened his eyes. "Holy shit! I did it!"

The pleased smile on her face matched his. "You're a natural, Keaton."

"Really?"

"Yep. Most witches can't conjure on their first attempt."

"I have to say, this is so freaking cool. What else can we do?"

She laughed and gave his forearm a light squeeze. "Same ol' Keaton. Still an overachiever after all these years."

A rueful grin curled his lips. "It's true. Give me an inch, and I'll take a mile."

"I remember," she said huskily.

The color of her eyes was not quite back to the warm, bright amber he remembered, but neither was it a muddy brown anymore. Since he'd learned about the color-changing irises of witches, he'd been paying attention to Autumn's moods. He appreciated the fact that she was letting go of the anger and hurt.

Trying to preserve the current mood, he tossed her the apple and closed his eyes. A cheerful, yellow daisy appeared mere seconds later. With a triumphant grin, he presented it to her with a flourish. "For you, m'lady."

"I love daisies."

"I know."

"You are too damned smooth for your own good," she grumbled good-naturedly as she swiped the flower from his hand.

He couldn't contain his laugh.

"Okay. Now we need winter clothes. See if you can conjure a parka in your size. If you want to try pushing it a step further, you can imagine it on your body."

It took three tries, but Keaton finally succeeded.

"Very good!" she cheered. "You'll be a pro in no time."

"I have an incredible teacher."

"Mmhmm. Your flattery won't work on me." She checked the clock. "We need to get a move on. You ready for this?"

"As I'll ever be."

"Okay, hold on."

"Oh, babe. You shouldn't tell me things like that. I'd like nothing more than to put my hands on your body."

Pink brightened her cheeks, and he chuckled as he shifted closer.

He wrapped her in a tight embrace. "Is this right?"

"Hand holding would do," she said dryly.

"But then I don't get to hug you close," he countered and nuzzled his lips against the hollow of her neck.

"You're pushing it, Keaton."

Since her tone remained light, he didn't let go. "I'm yours to whisk away."

Keaton experienced an internal warming. It started in his core and worked its way to his extremities. Right before the point of burning, it stopped. He hadn't been aware of closing his eyes or tightening his hold on Autumn, but when she tapped his shoulder and told him they'd arrived, he opened his eyes.

Sure enough, they stood along the edge of a wooded area. The tree-line extended a good three hundred yards beyond the exterior monastery wall. With great care, he released her and spun in a slow circle. "This is it?"

"This is it."

He nodded absently as he took in the view. In the distance, the snow-capped mountains stood majestically, crowned by a circle of low hanging, light-grey clouds—the perfect backdrop for the massive stone building before them.

"This is incredible," he breathed.

"It is," she agreed warmly.

He focused back on her and asked the question utmost in his mind. "Do you feel the infusion of heat when you teleport?"

"I do. That is your power ramping up." She placed a hand over the area of his solar plexus. "Magic starts on a cellular level and builds outward. Your body was responding to the power I was putting forth."

It made an odd sort of sense, and he nodded. "How is it done? How did we arrive here?"

"You concentrate on a mental image of where you are going. Preferably an open area so you don't wind up merged with a wall or tree."

He felt the color drain from his skin. "That can happen?"

"Yes, but not if you're careful. That's why it's important to have a clear picture in your mind."

"I thought I'd be more disoriented," he confessed.

"As a non-magical person, you might be. But like I said, your power responded to mine. It happens on occasion. I imagine your body's instincts took over."

"Okay, what's next?"

"We duck into the woods, conjure a couple of backpacks to complete our hiker disguise, and then make our way to the front doors on the north side of the building," she explained. "Once there, we create a cover story about losing our way. Hopefully, they will provide shelter for the night. It will give us a chance to snoop around."

"How did you become such an expert on this type of deception?"

She studied him for a minute then grinned. "I could tell you, but then I'd have to kill you."

He trudged into the woods behind her. "Couldn't we have been more James Bond-ish? Sweep in with some high-end toys, swipe the stone, and run out as the building explodes?"

"Bitch, bitch, bitch," she teased. "I'll tell you what, next mission, you get to concoct the plan."

"Deal."

CHAPTER 13

Chapter Thirteen has been omitted for obvious reasons. Consider this like a seventh-inning stretch. You can go hit up your social media accounts and tell everyone how awesome this story is.

CHAPTER 14

*T*he monastery was enormous. The golden temple rose five stories, with each level smaller in width than the first. The roof edges curled upwards as if smiling. Intricate floral carvings decorated the stone base and were at odds with the simplicity of the building design. Over the main entry was a black sign angled for ease of viewing for any visitors who cared to glance up. The sign contained two gold Chinese symbols that Autumn had no ability to translate. Similar smaller buildings dotted the landscape around them. The tall stone fence and iron gates created a compound feel.

She and Keaton were admitted to the monastery with minimal fuss. Their cover story didn't raise a brow. The silent group of Asian men studied them with solemn eyes.

One monk stood out among the rest. He was tinier than the others, standing only as tall as her shoulder. He wore a pleasant expression that bordered on jolly. The laugh lines in the corner of his eyes spoke of his happy disposition. Autumn dubbed him Jolly Ollie.

They were guided to separate rooms next door to each other. Autumn studied Keaton's room from the doorway as he laid his backpack on the thin cot-like bed in the corner of the small space. She needed a clear image of the room in the event of a teleport. His slight frown indicated he didn't understand her curiosity. She smiled mysteriously and followed Ollie to her equally tiny room.

"Do you speak English, Jolly Ollie?" she asked the man.

His eyes all but disappeared as they crinkled with laughter. Wordlessly, he bent at the waist and backed from the room.

"Not one for conversation, huh?" she called after the departing figure.

Within minutes, Keaton stood at her door. As a show of respect and per monastery rules, he didn't enter. "Not luxurious, but at least it's dry and somewhat warm. The scratchy wool blanket at the foot of the bed will come in handy tonight."

"True enough."

He checked the hallway and lowered his voice to ask, "What's the plan for searching?"

"I figure when the monks are in prayer this afternoon, it will be a good time to explore," she responded equally as soft.

He frowned and checked the hall again. "This place gives me the creeps."

Her head came up from where she'd been rummaging through her pack. A long time ago, she'd learned to trust her instincts. If Keaton's were screaming at him, something was off. "What's wrong? What do you feel?"

"Eyes. Everywhere."

She nodded. Yeah, she'd experienced the sensation too. "Did you feel a pull toward any particular direction when we entered?"

"The wing opposite these rooms."

"Me, too." She peered around him down the hall. "We'll head that way when we hear the mid-day prayer bell."

"How do you know so much about their schedule?"

"Alastair gave a detailed account to Summer this morning." She reached into her bra and pulled out the folded sheet of paper she'd tucked there before they left. With a triumphant grin, she held it up. "A map."

"Nice! Memorize it and hand it over."

She did as he suggested, but it took a while. The sheer size of the place was astounding. "Here. This is the area we passed through to get to this section of rooms. This…" She pointed to an area to the west of where they were. "…is where I felt the draw of something powerful. Magic has a pull. It makes sense that we would feel the stone if it's here."

He glanced down the hall again then turned his attention to the map. "Yeah, that location seems about right."

"You'd better head back to your room. Let's keep up appearances."

Keaton had barely tucked the map in his pocket when Ollie showed up and indicated they were to follow him. Together, they fell into line behind the monk.

"How long have you been here, Ollie?"

Her question didn't even garner a raised shoulder. With a side glance at Keaton, she quipped, "He's the strong, silent type. My favorite."

After a four-minute walk, they came to a large oak door off the great hall. Ollie knocked once and turned the handle. With another low bow, he waved an arm for them to enter the room. Without a word, he backed out and shut the door.

Across the twenty-foot space, a man with shiny blue-black hair dusted with gray stood looking out over the grounds. Although he appeared relaxed, Autumn received the impression he was, in fact, tense.

At roughly five-feet-ten, he was taller than the other monks. And while his Asian ancestry was obvious, his skin was a lighter shade of olive, and from her angle, his eyes appeared to be an odd, pale shade of green. It was as if the color had been leeched from his irises. There was no doubt this guy had mixed heritage.

They stood in silence for another full minute before Keaton cleared his throat.

When the man turned more fully, Autumn took an involuntary step backward. This was not a man to be trifled with. Call it instinct, or a warning from the Goddess, but every nerve ending screamed for her to run from this room and never return.

They stood locked in a staring contest. The malice in his eyes was unmistakable. Why he would possibly hate her was anyone's guess. Perhaps he despised women in general. And yet, she couldn't shake the feeling his animosity was personal somehow.

"Thank you for providing shelter for the evening," Keaton cut in smoothly drawing the man's attention from her. "I'm Keith Harrington, and this is my girlfriend, Amber Shaw."

Autumn released an internal sigh of relief that he had the forethought to lie. They hadn't discussed that part of the plan, but providing real names for the man across from them didn't seem wise.

A slight sneer lifted the man's lip before he smoothed all expression from his face. "I am Zhu Lin." There was no need for him to state his position. His air of command was apparent.

"Mr. Lin, thank you for your hospitality."

Autumn wasn't sure if it was her or the offer of thanks, but Lin's eyes darkened, and his expression hardened.

"You may stay tonight only. Tomorrow morning, you will be escorted outside the fence and sent on your way. While you are here, you will remain in your rooms when not dining." Lin didn't wait for a response to his decree before he moved behind his desk at the far end of the room. "You may go."

Temper on a low simmer, Autumn spun on her heel and headed for the exit. She paused in her retreat when Keaton didn't follow.

"You'll have to pardon me, Mr. Lin, but I don't understand your desire to be rid of us. Have we done something to offend?" Keaton asked, ever the politician.

With a squinting of his already narrow eyes, Lin shifted his gaze between Keaton and Autumn. "I don't care to have our routine disrupted, Mr. Harrington."

"I can well understand, sir. But the reason we sought shelter is because a storm is supposed to kick up in the province later today. It's not safe to be out in sub-zero temperatures."

A shrewd light entered Lin's gaze. To Autumn, it seemed a type of grudging respect for how well Keaton played the game. Lin gave a sharp nod and turned his attention to the tome in front of him.

"You may stay until the weather clears, but the same rules apply," Lin said. "Good day."

The door opened, and Ollie stood ready to usher them back to their rooms.

"KEATON! NO!"

The heavy urn Keaton had his hand inside crashed to the floor with a resounding boom. The echo throughout the stone chamber was deafening. They stood in stunned silence while they stared in horror at the shattered religious icon.

"What the hell can we do to fix this?" Keaton asked.

"Stand back."

Autumn didn't have time or the supplies to cast a circle, so she went with a quick incantation to protect herself before summoning up a spell she'd used once as a young teen. That time, like this, required the repair of a broken statue before she was caught.

As the pieces, large and small, rose in the air and swirled around them, Keaton ducked and squatted. "Careful, you almost took my ear off."

She didn't bother to respond, and instead, chose to concentrate on the task at hand.

Sandals slapped the stones in the corridor.

They were out of time.

With one last surge of energy, she fused the pieces together. A slight clink of metal hitting stone caught her attention. The Chintamani Stone, embedded in a hideous necklace design, fell at their feet. The wooden door slammed back on its hinges before she could retrieve the necklace.

An army of roughly fifteen short, heavyset monks flooded the room. One spoke rapid-fire in what she assumed was the Tibetan language.

Autumn looked to Keaton. "It's all Chinese to me," she quipped.

An inappropriate laugh escaped him, and he clasped her hand.

"Let's go. I don't think he's happy you performed magic on sacred ground."

She snapped her fingers.

Nothing happened.

Her heart rate kicked into high gear as she met Lin's smug pale-green gaze across the distance. The head honcho had a real chip on his naked right shoulder.

She snapped twice more in rapid succession.

"We're fucked," she croaked. "The room is warded against tele-porting."

As one, the monks surged toward them. Keaton fought fero-ciously but was no match for the other men. All of whom, it appeared, had been trained in hand-to-hand combat.

Autumn struggled against the hands holding her, using her magic to fling them off before another set landed on her again.

Within minutes, she was on the ground, her ribs smarting from the blows she took, and her wrists encircled in a pair of ancient-looking shackles with nearly illegible runes inscribed on the metal. She attempted to cast them off.

She was powerless.

Autumn had never been powerless in her entire life. She met Keaton's concerned gaze. Her own eyes must've reflected the terror she experienced at that moment, because he made one last-ditch effort to get to her before he was knocked unconscious.

The heels of his thick-soled boots dragged along the large, uneven stones as they hauled him toward the door.

"Where are you taking him?" she screamed. "*Keaton!*" She kicked out at the legs closest to her and twisted wildly against the arms holding her. "Where are you taking Keaton?"

"Is he a witch like you?"

Well, crap on a cookie! The man knew what she was.

She closed her eyes and shook her head at her stupidity. It explained the animosity.

"Then he will be spared."

Her eyes flew wide. Lin thought she meant Keaton was a non-magical human.

His words sunk in. *Spared?*

"Spared?"

"*If* he can find his way off the mountain."

"You sonofabitch! You can't throw him out in the snowstorm! He'll die!"

"Would you prefer he share your fate?"

She didn't know what her fate would be and was too terrified to ask.

"Take her to the dungeon."

"You *all* speak English?" As they hauled her to her feet, she stared down the man she'd dubbed Ollie. "Way to be a tool, Ollie."

A spark of humor flashed in his rheumy dark eyes, but he quickly turned serious. The abrupt change confused her. It was as if he were amused by her and yet trying to relay a message at the same time.

"Ms. Thorne."

Her heart jerked to a stop when the monks halted her in her tracks. They shifted her to face Lin.

"If you pray, you may want to spend tonight in prayer. Tomorrow, you burn."

Did she want to know what he meant? She gulped and croaked out the question.

"Where do you think the tradition of executing witches arose?" he mocked.

"Do you want the long, technical version? I've done a lot of research. Nothing indicated Buddhist monks were in on the craze though."

"A well-placed word or suggestion and our will is done."

"*Your* will, you mean. The rest of your monk minions are mindless asshats," she retorted. "But really, what do you have against a poor harmless witch? I've done nothing to you."

"But your family has."

Okay, *that* sounded ominous.

"Take her."

"Can't we talk about this," she called over her shoulder. "I'm great at setting things to rights. I mean look what I did in here. It's cleaner than when I started."

A choked snigger sounded to her left. She gave Ollie an odd look.

"At least someone has a sense of humor," she muttered.

They descended a trillion stairs and followed a tunnel for what seemed like miles. Finally, when Autumn was certain she would drop from exhaustion, they reached their destination.

The smell of decaying flesh and feces nearly gagged her.

Real fear clawed at the back of her throat and made it difficult to swallow.

"Yeah, no. I'm not staying down here. It's not sanitary," she croaked out.

Again, Ollie choked off a laugh. It earned him a glaring reprimand from his more serious companion. Ollie grabbed a nearby torch resting in a holder on the stone wall. He held it aloft while Mr. Stern worked a key in the rusted padlock.

"That's pretty old. It's probably not going to work," she babbled and eased back a few steps. "I'll tell you what. You release me, and I'll disappear. I promise neither me nor any future Thornes will bother any of you again."

The ancient lock disengaged, and Mr. Stern jerked his chin at the now open doorway.

The smell triggered her gag reflex and tears streamed from her eyes. "Please," she begged.

Autumn was only tough to an extent. The idea of being locked in a dark room with Goddess-knew-what type of rotting things residing there petrified her to the extreme.

Ollie walked in and lit another torch inside what was, in fact, an oversized stone cell.

Mr. Stern shoved her hard enough to make her stagger.

When she righted herself, she screamed. Not just any scream. It was the type of bloodcurdling scream to bring down walls and shatter windows. Later, if she lived, she'd pride herself on how long and loud the sound was. Horror movie worthy, in fact.

A fist slammed into her jaw. The excruciating pain nearly caused her to black out. Holy crap! How did MMA fighters take that kind of abuse and still remain upright?

The blow knocked her into the nearest wall. Bones and chains clanked together and triggered another terrified scream. Rough hands jerked her sideways. The shackles binding her hands along with her powers were attached onto another chain. The position forced her arms above her head and was more painful than she could've imagined—had she ever thought to imagine it. In no time, her shoulders would ache, fatigue would set in, and she'd lose feeling in her limbs. No doubt, that's what the design intended.

Her breaths came in rapid little pants, and she feared she'd hyperventilate.

"Please, Ollie. Don't leave me here. Please."

Ollie cast her one last long, regretful look, bent low, and backed out the door.

"Ollie! Please! Please, Ollie," she sobbed.

Soon snot and tears poured unchecked down her face.

"Goddess, if you hear me, please help me," she cried over and over until she was hoarse and exhausted.

Minutes, then hours, crawled by. There was no way to block out the smell or the horror of the space. The blackened eye sockets of various skulls grew and receded in the flickering torchlight. The mouths of the dead gaped open in terror or pain. How long had they been made to suffer? She supposed she'd be spared the indignity of their fate when they burned her.

Worn out, with nothing left to do, she dozed. A scratching noise penetrated her subconscious and brought her to an abrupt waking state. Heart pounding, she listened.

Did the shadows in the corner move?

When a shape emerged from the corner, she screamed for all she was worth.

CHAPTER 15

*B*itter cold penetrated Keaton's unconscious state and urged his brain into immediate wakefulness. His teeth repeatedly slammed together in an uncontrolled chatter. Good Christ, he was cold. He wondered if the furnace in their house had gone out.

Chloe! She had to be freezing.

He opened his eyes and stared at the dawning sun.

Confusion set in. Where was he? How did he come to be on the side of a mountaintop in this inclement weather?

The pounding in his brain wouldn't allow him to piece together why he lay in a snowbank outside a large castle-like wall. There was something he needed to remember, and if his damned teeth would stop moving long enough for him to think, he could.

Boots appeared in his peripheral.

"Are you done with your nap, boy?"

Keaton inched his head up to view the owner of the boots. Memories flooded back.

"Alastair Thorne."

"Where's my niece?"

With great care, Keaton turned his head to look in the direction of the monastery. "I don't know what they did with her."

"Were you not with her?"

"There were too many of them," Keaton ground out as he eased up from his prone position. He took exception to the insinuation that he'd left her to her fate. "I was knocked out."

"Useless. The whole damned Carlyle clan. Not a one of you with a lick of sense among you," Alastair ranted. "Tell me you at least got the stone."

Keaton's brows hit his hairline. "We have no idea if Autumn is dead or alive, and you're worried about the fucking stone?"

"So you didn't get it," Alastair concluded with a sneer. "Why am I not surprised?"

If every muscle in Keaton's body wasn't cramped and in excruciating pain, he'd beat the pompous prick to a pulp. *"Fuck. You!"* was the best he could manage through his chattering teeth.

The blond warlock studied him for a long moment. His expression changed from angry disgust to long-suffering. "I suppose my niece will be irate with me if I leave you to freeze to death." With a snap of his fingers, Alastair restored warmth to Keaton's limbs.

Keaton was able to unfold his arms enough to grab his pounding head.

"Stand up, useless boy. Let me see."

As he clamped down on his tongue to prevent the building tirade, Keaton rose and shifted.

"Jaw and temple. Perhaps you didn't go down without a fight. Stand still."

Alastair removed the black leather glove from his left hand. He placed glowing fingertips to Keaton's pounding temple. All pain ebbed away in a slow trickle.

"Better?"

"Much." It was hard to force out the *thank you*, but he managed.

"Tell me everything that led up to your face-plant in the snow," Alastair ordered.

When Keaton was finished relaying the details of their showdown with the ninja monks, he asked, "Do you have any ideas on how to get her back? The head honcho, Lin, had a magic-busting trick or two up his sleeve."

"It's like Lin knew she was coming," Alastair mused.

"Or at the very least, knew what she was when we showed up."

"Yes." Autumn's uncle eyed him in speculation. "You're sure you don't know what happened to the stone after Lin charged the room?"

Keaton shook his head and shrugged. "Sorry."

A spark of something resembling amusement lit the older man's dark-blue eyes. "Mmm. Well, let's stage a rescue, shall we?"

"How do you plan to do that?"

"Quiet."

Alastair closed his eyes and tilted his head as if listening for a specific sound.

Keaton thought the guy was a few Fruit Loops shy of a full bowl, but he wasn't going to piss off the powerful warlock.

"This way."

"Uh, Alastair? That's *away* from the monastery."

"If you are going to question every decision, you can stay behind. I'll send Autumn back for you if the cold doesn't get you first."

After five minutes of walking in the sub-zero temps, Keaton spoke up again. "Can't you just, you know, blink us there or something?"

Alastair halted and whirled, leaning forward until he was practically nose to nose with Keaton. "You're a powerful magical being. Quit whining and start acting like one."

"How do you suggest I warm myself, huh?" Keaton snapped in turn. "I must've missed that particular class."

"Your parents should be shot for neglecting their duty to you. Perhaps if you'd have been raised properly, you wouldn't have broken my dear niece's heart."

"Dear niece? Ha! She can't stand you. And don't you dare threaten my parents!"

Alastair laughed in straight-up amusement. "I noticed you didn't deny breaking Autumn's heart."

"No. I'll own up to my part."

"Good. I like you a smidgeon better now. Which isn't saying much." Alastair rubbed his hands together. "Okay, to warm yourself, you need to build the warmth from the nucleus of each cell."

Keaton hung his head. For fuck's sake, he was never going to be warm again.

"Pay attention, boy. I'm trying to help you," Alastair growled. "I don't have all damned day." He sneezed, froze for a second, then fisted his hand. "Bloody locust," he muttered.

"What the hell was that chirping sound?" Keaton asked, whipping his head back and forth to pinpoint where it came from.

"Never you mind. Close your eyes and concentrate." Alastair placed the flat of his hand on Keaton directly above his stomach. "Here. Everything you do is done from your solar plexus. Imagine a warm ball of light. Can you visualize it?"

Keaton nodded.

"Good. Pull that ball into you. Here, where my hand is. Do you have it?"

"Yes."

"Okay, now imagine that ball growing, shooting its light through to your head, hands, and toes. Feel the warmth building?"

Keaton's eyes flew wide. "Yes!"

"Keep that ball pulsing in your core as you walk. You'll stay warm."

Other than the initial surge of power when his parents had removed the spell that bound his powers, Keaton had never felt the magic as strongly. "Did you do that? Create that energy?"

Alastair smiled with what Keaton imagined, for him, was genuine warmth. "No, son, that was all you. Well done."

The smile froze and dropped from his face. Once again, Alastair tilted his head as if to listen. "They know we're here. Place your hand on my shoulder, and whatever you do, do not let go." He mumbled an incantation in what Keaton assumed was Latin. "Walk in my footprints and don't make a sound."

Men rushed into the wooded area and surrounded them.

Unfazed, Alastair held a finger to his lips with one hand and pointed forward with the other.

Keaton painstakingly placed each foot in the hollowed-out footprints Alastair left in front of him. A glance behind showed no indentation at all. It was slow moving, but the other men didn't seem to know the two of them were there. *How the hell was that even possible?* If they got to their destination alive, he planned to find out.

Soon enough, they were beyond the tree line, and the army of crazy, ninja monks was behind them still searching the woods.

"You can speak now, but be careful to keep your voice low," Alastair told him. "You may let go of me."

Keaton was loathe to do so. He'd never admit it, but there was a comfort in touching the warlock, as if the guy had a magical force field that would protect him from all things.

"Perhaps one day, I'll teach you how to create the shield," Alastair said as if he'd read Keaton's mind.

The fucker was eerie.

"Thanks," he mumbled.

"The entrance should be close. Look for a marking that resembles a dragon. It will be carved into the trunk of a large tree." Alastair grabbed his arm before he wandered away. "Boy, I don't need to tell you to be stealthy. If you are caught, I'm leaving you here. Do you understand?"

"Yes."

"Good. Find the dragon."

"It seems I already have," he snarked.

Alastair's chuckle rumbled around them. "Careful, I'm starting to like you."

It took roughly five minutes, but Keaton discovered what could only be described as the carved dragon Alastair was referring to. "I found it," he called softly.

"Stay there, and when I tell you, place your hand in his mouth."

Apprehension chased up Keaton's spine and burned as the tension built in the back of his neck. "Am I going to lose a hand?"

Alastair snorted his amusement. "I hope not, but I've never entered this way before."

Keaton shot him a sharp glance. "You've been inside this hellhole?"

"Once, a long time ago. Be ready." He moved around another tree. "Ah, here it is. Okay, slowly place your hand inside the mouth."

Keaton inched the fingers of his right hand inside the hole. Sweat pooled on his lower back. He realized too late that he should've used his left hand. In the event he had to gnaw his arm off at the wrist, he'd still have use of his primary hand.

"Oh, boy?"

He froze as Alastair's voice drifted to him. "Yeah?"

"Think positive thoughts. Anything else might cost you a limb."

Keaton shoved aside the daydream of murdering Alastair and worked on blanking his mind. Thank God—er, the Goddess— Autumn taught him meditation in order to purify himself for their lessons.

A loud scraping sounded, and the ground shook beneath him.

It was an effort, but he tamped down his dismay.

Alastair appeared at his side. "You can remove your hand. Good job. Come."

They descended stairs that looked like they'd been carved into the earth centuries before. Some were more worn than others. Moss partially covered nearly all the steps and made the journey to the bottom treacherous.

"You couldn't tell me the whole positive-thought thing *before* I shoved my hand in the hole?" Keaton asked.

"Where's the fun in that?"

"Christ, you *are* Autumn's uncle."

"Was there ever any doubt?"

Alastair halted before what looked to be an ordinary stone wall.

Keaton cursed. "It's a dead end. What the fuck?"

"Ye of little faith. Pay attention, boy, you may learn something."

"Will you stop calling me boy? I'm thirty-two years old. Hardly a boy."

Alastair gave him one solid hit on the back with the flat of his hand. "To me, you'll always be a boy. Now, can you shut up for more than five minutes to allow me to figure this out?"

Alastair held out a hand and created a miniature ball of light similar to the one he had Keaton visualize. The chamber lit.

"Brush off the dirt there."

Keaton did what he was told and swiped his hand across the ancient stone to his left.

Alastair held the light closer to read the symbols. They must have made sense to the older man because he nodded and strode toward the corner of the room. He counted the blocks down from the top and shot a delighted grin Keaton's way.

"This feels like we're part of Raiders of the Lost Ark, doesn't it?"

Keaton returned his grin. "It sort of does."

"Come on, boy. Time to save the girl!"

Alastair pressed a stone to his right.

This time, Keaton understood the scraping noise for what it was —*a secret passage.*

"I cannot go in there or my magic will be neutralized," Alastair told him with a quick check of their surroundings. He reached into his pocket and pulled out a skeleton key. "This will unlock the shackles."

"How did you—?"

"Never you mind, son. Get in there and get her out. I'll keep guard." Alastair gave him a shove. "Go."

Keaton stepped into the cell and let his eyes adjust. He didn't have time to register his surroundings before a bloodcurdling scream nearly pierced his eardrums.

"Jesus, Autumn! It's me!"

"Keaton? *Ohmygod,* Keaton!" she sobbed.

"Shhh, babe. I'm here. It's okay." The rancid smell of the room caught up with him. "What the hell is that—holy fucking shitballs! Are these…?" He trailed off as he looked at the dead bodies chained to the walls around them.

Her ragged sobs brought his attention back to her. Keaton squatted in front of her and cupped her face. "Babe, look at me."

Her eyes darted around as if she feared the bodies would come back to life at any second.

"Autumn, love, look at me. Just at me."

She turned frantic eyes on him.

"That's my brave sweetheart. I've got the key, and I'm going to get you out of here, okay?"

"O-okay."

Although his skin was crawling under the hollow gazes of the dead, he managed to keep an upbeat tone as he worked the lock of her shackles. "You're never going to guess who I ran into."

"Wh-who?"

"Uncle Alastair."

"Uncle Alastair?"

"Yep. And he taught me a nifty little trick to stay warm." He shot her a reproachful glance. "One you should've taught me before we came to this god-forsaken place."

Her eyes darted around, and she swallowed convulsively.

"Babe, I know this macabre setting is creepy as hell, but I'm going to need you to stay focused on me, all right?"

"All r-right."

"Almost got it."

"Hurry!" Alastair hissed from the opening.

"I'm trying!" Keaton barked. "This damned lock must be three hundred years old."

"Older, but try faster."

Alastair ducked his head back out, leaving them alone.

"If he hadn't saved my ass, I'd deck him. I swear."

"H-he saved you?"

"Yeah. He didn't have to, but he mentioned something about you being upset with him if he didn't."

Autumn smiled through her tears.

"There's my beautiful sweetheart. Welcome back." He dropped a kiss on her forehead. The lock clicked, and he peeled the shackles from her wrists. "Let's not hang out, huh?"

She shook her arms and moaned her pain.

"I'm going to carry you, babe. If you have some type of spell to make yourself featherlight, I'd appreciate it."

Autumn took a few precious seconds to hug him. "I can walk. It's only my arms and shoulders that hurt."

"Good, let's get the hell out of Dodge before Lin and his buddies return."

They'd cleared the doorway as he finished his sentence. As if Keaton had conjured him, Lin appeared, gun in hand.

"I thought if I imprisoned one of your own, you'd show up, Thorne."

"Well, I do hate to disappoint," Alastair drawled. He shifted to stand in front of Autumn and reached a hand back to her.

Keaton felt Autumn grip his hand, and from the corner of his eye saw her slip hers into her uncle's.

"I swore if you ever returned, I would kill you."

"You always were so bloodthirsty, Lin. And here I thought we were pals."

"Hand me the Chintamani Stone, and I will make it quick."

Alastair gave a careless shrug. "That's just the thing, my old friend. I don't have it. Seems neither do you, huh? On that note…"

With a snap of the fingers of his free hand, Alastair transported them all to the Thorne estate.

Keaton almost fell to his knees in gratitude. If it wouldn't have looked uncool, he'd have kissed the ground. Instead, he hauled Autumn into his embrace.

"I never thought I'd see you again," she cried.

"You can't get rid of me that easily, babe."

"No thanks, necessary," Alastair inserted dryly.

Autumn drew back and faced her uncle.

Keaton didn't know what to expect, but Autumn flinging herself into Alastair's embrace wasn't quite it.

"Thank you, Uncle."

The older man closed his eyes and held her tight. "You're welcome, child." He pulled back and smoothed a hand down her hair. With his chin, he nodded to Keaton. "Teach this one how to survive, huh?"

"Yes, sir."

"I'll be in touch soon. We need to discuss the necklace your boyfriend lifted."

"He didn't…" She faced Keaton. "Did you?"

Keaton grinned and opened the collar of his shirt.

Alastair's laughter echoed around them. "Like I said, I'll be in touch."

CHAPTER 16

"*I* can't seem to get the smell of death out of my nose," Autumn complained a short while later. She'd taken a long, hot shower and scrubbed herself from head to toe—*twice*.

Keaton had been sprawled out on the living room couch. He sat up as she crossed the room. "I know. I've rinsed out the inside of each nostril twice and sniffed a can of coffee grounds in hopes of neutralizing the smell."

Her shudder wasn't fake.

He rose and opened his arms. "Come here, babe."

Because she needed the comfort, Autumn allowed him to cuddle her close.

"Are you truly okay?" he asked softly as he rubbed his cheek against the crown of her head.

"I think so." She swallowed hard in an effort not to cry. "I feel like such a wimp."

He drew back a few inches to meet her tearful gaze. "Are you kidding me? You were a fucking warrior! Not only did you fight like a woman possessed, you withstood God knows how many hours in that pit of hell."

"Goddess," she murmured the correction.

"Yeah, that term is taking me time to come to grips with. Old habits die hard and all." He scooped her up into his arms and sank down on the seat cushion. "I was terrified for you. Then when I saw you in that cell, chained like that..." He shook his head and swallowed audibly.

"I know."

"I'm not sure you do," he said, squeezing her harder.

"I do," she insisted. "When you were knocked out, I went a little insane. Lin said they intended to throw you out in the blizzard. All I could think was that you had no way to protect yourself from the elements and that you'd freeze."

"I froze my balls off. But luckily enough, Alastair showed up."

"Well, as long as it was only your balls that froze off, I guess that's okay," she said with a slight smile.

"Don't talk about my boys like that. If they hear you, they will shrivel to nothing in memory of the bitter cold."

She laughed and rested her head against his chest. A few moments passed in comfortable silence before she spoke. "Thank you for coming back for me."

"Always."

Tears burned the back of her lids. "Lin was going to reenact the Salem witch trials."

His arms jerked then tightened. "Good Christ!"

"Keaton?"

"Mmm?"

She took a deep breath and charged forward with her request. "Will you stay with me tonight?" The tension lining his body could be felt under her hand. Misgivings assailed her, and she backtracked. "You don't have to. I just... it's just... never mind."

"I can't."

Her heart spasmed, and she imagined she heard the crack as it broke again. "Yeah, that's okay—"

"No, I mean I can't stay with you and not want something more, Autumn."

She shrugged. "Sex is good. I'm okay with sex." Gah! She sounded like an idiot.

"That's good to know." Amusement deepened his voice. "But what I meant was that I love you, and I want to start over again."

This time, she was the one who froze. Was she ready to go there a second time? While it hurt her heart to have her invitation rejected, she hadn't planned what to do after the one night.

"Babe?"

She remained quiet as she gathered her scattered thoughts.

The large hand rubbing her back stopped, and she felt Keaton's withdrawal like it was a living thing.

"I'm scared," she finally admitted.

"Me, too."

Any response she would've made was cut off by the arrival of her sisters and Coop. Instinctively, she tugged Keaton's collar closed to hide the amulet with the Chintamani Stone. Her eyes lifted to his, but he didn't voice the question in his eyes.

"You're back!" Summer cried happily. Her sister was two steps into the room when she realized the wrongness of the energy. "What happened? Why do you look like you both went ten rounds in an MMA ring? Should I call Aunt GiGi?"

Autumn held up a hand as she climbed from Keaton's lap. "One question at a time, okay?"

"Don't keep us in suspense, sister," Winnie said as she graced Autumn with a hug.

Spring and Summer embraced her in turn, each careful to avoid squeezing too hard in deference to her battered body.

Keaton spoke up, giving a play-by-play account of their time in the Himalayas.

"I've never heard of shackles to make a witch powerless," Summer said after he'd finished. "Do you remember what the runes looked like? Could you draw a few? Maybe we can figure out what to do if we encounter them again."

Autumn shrugged. "I could try. But the main thing I'd like to know is why Zhu Lin hates our family. Something to do with Alastair, I'm sure."

"I've never even heard the name before today," Winnie said. She shared a glance with her other sisters who shook their heads to indicate they hadn't either.

"Well, someone knows about him," Coop said grimly. "I intend to find out."

"He knew who and what I was. It makes me think he's been keeping tabs on our family," Autumn said. "He's not a man to cross."

"We'll figure it out. Perhaps Dad has answers." Spring rose gracefully to her feet. "In the meantime, I'll whip up a batch of Aunt GiGi's health elixir for you and Keaton."

"Ugh, no! Please! That stuff tastes like dirt," Autumn complained.

"Health elixir?" Keaton asked as he shifted to place an arm around her waist.

Autumn smiled inside as all three of her sisters' gazes bugged out due to Keaton's gesture. "My aunt swears it cures what ails you."

"If it takes away my body aches, I'm all for it," Keaton said.

In all the confusion, she'd forgotten he'd taken a hard blow to the head. She twisted to face him and ran her hands through his hair, examining his scalp. "How's the head?"

"Fine. Alastair took care of it right after he showed up."

"That makes me feel somewhat better. He's nothing if not thorough."

Keaton gathered her hands in his and kissed her knuckles. "I'm fine, babe. Promise."

She took him at his word and faced her sisters. "I'm exhausted. Neither of us has really slept in nearly thirty-six hours. Can any other questions wait until after we get some rest?"

"Of course." Winnie urged her to head upstairs. "You can take my room if you'd like. I'll bring up a glass of Aunt GiGi's medicine."

"Thanks, but I can conjure new sheets for my old bed. It will only take a second, and I don't want to run you out of your room,"

Autumn told her tiredly. She cast one last glance at Keaton and headed toward the stairs.

"I need sleep, too," she heard Keaton say. "Good night."

As she reached the bottom of the stairs, his arms came around her. "I thought you wanted me to stay?" he asked for her ears alone.

"I do. But I can't make promises about the future."

He studied her for a moment then nodded slowly. "Then let me hold you tonight and chase away your demons."

Because gratefulness stole her voice, she simply nodded and clasped his hand. Together, they climbed the stairs toward her old room.

AUTUMN FELL ASLEEP THE SECOND HER HEAD HIT THE PILLOW. BUT as tired as he was, sleep eluded Keaton. After what felt like a lifetime of want, he finally had the love of his life in his arms again, and he didn't care to waste a minute of it sleeping.

The soft knock on the door didn't disturb Autumn, and for that, Keaton was grateful. She'd been through a trauma and needed the rest.

"Come in," he called out softly.

The door inched open, and Winnie peeked her head in. "I've brought you the drink," she whispered as she set it on the nightstand.

"Thanks," he whispered in return.

"I've only seen her like this one other time. How bad was it really?"

"Pretty fucking horrible. They practically entombed her in the dungeon." He smoothed back Autumn's thick hair and caressed the shell of her ear. "She tried to be so brave, Winnie." He raised tortured eyes. "There were dead bodies and rats. I was only in there a few minutes, and I can't seem to get the smell out of my nose or the horror out of my mind. She was there for hours."

Tears welled in Winnie's eyes, and she placed a hand over her lips.

"They intended to burn her for being a witch," he growled in remembered anger. "If I ever get Lin alone, I'll kill him."

Winnie's soft hand touched his shoulder. "Thank you for taking care of her."

As she started to leave, he called out. "The other time? When was that?"

Her pale-blue eyes clouded, and she grimaced. "The day you broke up with her." She stared at her sleeping sister and brushed away a tear that had fallen. "She loved you with every fiber of her being, Keaton. About a week after she found you and Diane, she showed up here a virtual shell of her former self. I don't know that my sister has ever fully come back to us." Winnie focused her attention on him. "She acts tough, and for the most part she is, but I think you still have the power to destroy her. Please don't."

"I've never stopped loving her, Winnie. Not for one second of one day," he confessed, and even to his own ears his voice sounded rough. "Sure, I was angry and felt betrayed by her confession and by the spell she cast, but there was never a time I didn't love her."

"You had a funny way of showing it."

"I was a dumbass and didn't appreciate the gift the Goddess had given me. I won't make that mistake again."

"See that you don't," she said sternly. "Drink the potion. You'll feel better soon."

"I'm always a little leery of eating or drinking anything from any of you," he confessed with an apologetic smile.

Wicked amusement brightened her eyes, and a grin tugged at her lips. While her coloring was different from her sister, Winnie never resembled Autumn more than in that moment. "I'd find a much more creative ending for you, my friend."

"You women are scary. Anyone ever told you that?"

Her light, musical laughter followed her from the room.

He chuckled and reached for the drink then grimaced at the taste.

"I told you it tasted like dirt," Autumn said from her side of the bed.

"You did," he agreed with a smile. "I thought you were sleeping."

"I was but…" She shrugged. "I'm finding it difficult to get the image of that cell out of my head—even in sleep."

"What can I do?"

"You're doing it," she assured him. "I don't want to be alone."

"I'll stay as long as you need me to." He rested his head on the pillow and traced the outline of her face. "How much did you hear?"

"All of it. My sister has a big mouth."

"Don't be cross with her. She has your best interests at heart."

Autumn gave him a sardonic half-smile. "It's the only reason I'm not turning her into a frog."

"Can you do that? I mean, is it something a witch or warlock can actually do?"

She laughed and leaned forward to drop a kiss on his lips. "You're so cute."

"That's not an answer."

"If you ever come across that particular spell in your family's grimoire, be sure to let me know."

"Don't think I'm not going to look for it. If only to know how to turn myself back into a human," he joked.

All humor left her, and she searched his face. For what, he didn't know. "I love you, too, Keaton. I don't know that I ever stopped."

His heart slowed before it kicked into overdrive. "Why are you telling me this now? Especially after you said you weren't sure about rekindling what we had?"

"I don't want to rekindle what we had."

And just like that, his heart plummeted to his stomach. He rolled on his back and stared at the ceiling. How many times did she have to slam it home that she didn't want him? He was a fool.

"Keaton, look at me."

He dragged his gaze back to her face.

"I don't want to rekindle what we had. I want to start fresh. With you."

A frown pulled at his brow. He wasn't sure whether he was

hearing what he wanted to or not. "You want to start a new relationship with me? Forget the past?"

She nodded and offered a tremulous smile. "I do."

"Yes. A million times, yes!"

Her beaming smile propelled him forward and over top of her.
She fell back with a laugh and raised her head to meet him halfway
for their shared kiss.

He tugged her t-shirt over her head and sighed his pleasure. It
had been a long while since he'd seen her beautiful creamy breasts.
The sight of the pebbled nipples delighted him.

"I missed you, ladies."

She laughed and shimmied out of her pajama shorts.

After Autumn was completely naked, Keaton took his time
studying and touching all the places he'd dreamed about. He trailed
the tips of his fingers along her collarbone, ran them over the smooth
curve of her breast. Leaning down, he licked the tight bud and blew
softly before fastening onto the tip and suckling her.

Autumn's deep moan of pleasure spurred Keaton on. He became
more aggressive in his sucking and scraped his teeth along her sensitive skin. She rewarded him with another throaty groan as she dug
her fingers into the back of his skull to hold him close.

Without warning, she rolled, reversing their positions and putting
herself on top.

Keaton reached up to cup her. He kneaded the fullness even as he
jackknifed into a sitting position to capture her lips with his. He felt
her shift to completely straddle his hips. When she rubbed her slick
core against his straining erection, he released a low gasp.

"Oh, babe," he groaned. "You don't know what you do to me."

"I have some idea," she purred as she guided his fingers to her
wetness.

Having her take control by using his hand to pleasure herself was
sexy as hell. Keaton curled his fingers into her and inserted his
middle digit into her hot, sleek opening. He slowly pumped in and
out as he continued to taste the various areas of her silky skin. The
hollow of her throat was a particular favorite of his.

As Autumn's breathing hitched, Keaton drew back to watch her reaction to his caresses. Their eyes connected. Hers blazed with need.

With his thumb, he flicked the nub of her clit. Her eyes widened, then narrowed with intent. This time when she rolled, he was prepared. He held her arms straight out from her sides. Flat on her back, legs sprawled wide, she resembled a sacrifice. His sacrifice.

He grinned with delight and dropped slow, lingering kisses along the slight curve of her belly. When he reached her mound, he shot her a wink and dove in to taste her. With a desperate cry, she lifted her hips to meet his mouth.

"Yes!" she moaned. "Goddess, yes!"

Keaton toyed with her, working her into a state of incoherent need. But before he could bury himself into her warmth, she disappeared.

"What the fuck?"

Laughter sounded behind him, and he twisted around. There she stood, in all her naked glory, naughtiness dancing in her bright golden eyes.

"Your turn," she said huskily. "Flat on your back, big boy."

His dick twitched with her throaty chuckle, and he quickly complied.

Inch by inch she crawled up his body and, with her fingertips, used magic to heat his skin. There was no pain, only a fire that burned within to match her power.

"What is that? Why do I feel...?" He had no words and shook his head in frustration.

"Our magic is reaching out to connect. Amazing isn't it?"

His blood pounded through his veins as the magic pulsed in his body, looking to connect with hers. He'd never experienced a more erotic moment than when she wrapped her palm around his cock and licked the tip.

"Christ, Autumn!"

"Just wait," she laughed before taking him fully into her mouth.

His balls contracted, and the orgasm started. Keaton closed his eyes and tangled his fingers in her long auburn hair. But before he could ejaculate, her other hand cupped his balls, and whatever magic she produced, stopped him from coming.

His eyes flew wide, and he stared at her in disbelief.

The wicked gleam in her gaze preceded her dipping her head and licking him from base to tip. "I'm not ready for you to get off yet."

"How did you...?"

"Don't ask. Feel."

And feel he did. Every stroke of her tongue. Every pull of her lips. Even the length of him in her mouth, touching the back of her throat. It all worked him into a frenzy until he was thrusting into her mouth harder than he should've but unable to control the instinctive movement. Once again his balls contracted, and once again she halted his orgasm.

"God, I can't take this, babe," he ground out.

"You can, and you will." She retorted. "Now fuck me, Keaton." She positioned a pillow under her stomach and reclined forward on her elbow. "Fuck me like you mean it. Like you can't get enough. Like I'm your one and only."

He could no longer feel his face. All the blood in his body had pooled into his dick, making his raging hard-on throb. When he eased into her, she sighed her pleasure.

"Harder."

He drew back and pumped with more force.

"Harder."

Soon, he was pistoning in and out with little finesse, burying himself as deep as possible. She didn't seem to mind, in fact, she encouraged him with every mew of pleasure she released.

Her orgasm came in the form of her contracting walls and a burning heat wrapping around him. No longer able to hold back, he gripped her hip in one hand as he wrapped an arm around her waist. Three more hard thrusts had him following her over the edge.

They collapsed in a heap of arms and legs.

When he could draw in enough air to speak, he gasped her name.

She smiled and kissed him gently. "I'll give you five minutes to recover, and then we go again."

"You're trying to kill me," he complained with a caress of her hip.

"Nope. Just trying to make up for lost time."

"In that case, give me three minutes and I'm all yours."

"You are such a team player."

"That's me," he managed between pants. "Mr. MVP."

CHAPTER 17

"*I* need to head home, babe. Chloe will be waking soon, and I should be there for her," Keaton said to the woman sprawled across his naked body.

"Mmm."

He grinned. Autumn had never been a morning person, and it looked like nothing had changed in the interim since they'd been lovers.

He ran a hand down the length of her body, caressing and exploring the curves and smooth texture of her skin. When he got to her ass, he cupped it and sighed. Even after a full night of incredible sex, his joystick decided it was ready to go another round.

A quick glance at the clock curtailed that idea. He needed to be home for his daughter.

"You're holding onto my ass like you're afraid to let go," Autumn mumbled against his chest.

"I am," he said with a sigh and a squeeze of her full cheek. "I'm afraid this is all a dream, and when I wake up, you'll still hate me."

She lifted up on crossed arms and stared into his face. "Not likely. But I could go with you and then the three of us could grab breakfast at Monica's."

"I love that idea. Can you get a shower in five minutes?"

"If you promise to conjure me a cup of coffee."

He stopped stroking her ass. "Am I ready to conjure hot liquids?" Unsure why the thought made him nervous, he decided perhaps he should dress so he didn't burn his dick and balls off in the event he fucked up.

Autumn rose up, straddled his lap, and wound her fingers in his hair. With a not so gentle tug, she pulled his head back so he was gazing up into her bright amber eyes. "You'd be surprised what you are ready for. I have faith you can do that and more. If you can think it, it can be done."

His heart hammered with excitement and some other unnamed emotion. Dread? The combination of the two felt odd.

"You can do it, Keaton. It's all about visualization. The cup, the liquid, even how close to the rim you want the coffee and the condiments inside. Build it in your mind."

Keaton steadied his nerves and held out his hand. First, came the mug. Then came the hot coffee, and next, a teaspoon of sugar. Lastly, he visualized a dash of vanilla creamer. When he opened his eyes, the perfect cup of coffee was in his grasp, and Autumn sat beaming like a proud parent.

"Now stir it up. Water is your sign, and coffee is mostly water. Swirl it to stir the sugar and cream," she instructed.

Recalling what she'd taught him about gently pushing the magic instead of pulsing, he created movement of the liquid.

"Perfect, now draw back before you create a coffee tidal wave," she laughed.

He presented her with the conjured cup of coffee. "Five minutes."

After a quick sip of her drink, Autumn sighed her pleasure. "I think we can start teaching you the fundamentals of teleporting soon."

The idea had appeal, and Keaton nodded his agreement. "I'd like that."

"Good. You can head home so you won't be late, and I'll pop over shortly."

Keaton cast another regretful glance at the clock. Left with no choice, he climbed from the bed and started to dress.

"Last night was amazing," he told her as he drew his jeans up over his hips and arranged himself inside his pants.

The satisfied curl of her lips caused his own to curl.

"It was. Thank you, Keaton. For effectively making me forget, and for... you know, the rest."

He sighed with regret when she covered her ample curves with a robe. "Entirely my pleasure, babe. I love you."

"I love you, too." They stared, neither wanting to break contact. "You should go."

"I should."

Another long pause passed before she rose up on her knees on the mattress's edge.

Keaton stepped forward until their bodies were pressing together. "If I could, I'd stay in this moment forever."

"I know. Chloe is lucky to have such a devoted dad."

"Thank you for that. Over the years, I've wondered if I've provided all she needs. Diane has certainly not been a help."

Autumn snorted. "She wouldn't be. All her attention is on boinking Pastor Graves."

"What?"

"It's not important."

"It most certainly is," he argued.

Her darkening frown should've warned him of the coming storm. "Why?"

"What do you mean, why? She's the mother of my child." How could she not see this reflected on him?

"If she means nothing to you, then you shouldn't be upset."

"I didn't say she meant nothing to me, Autumn. She—"

Without a word, Autumn disappeared into thin air.

"The fuck?" He spun around and caught a flash of auburn hair in

143

the bathroom. With an irritated sigh, he strode into the adjoining space. "What the hell was that about?"

"Go home, Keaton." The cold tone of her voice left him in little doubt of her anger.

"No. You don't get to do this. Whatever slight, real or imagined, we need to talk about."

"You want to talk? Fine. We'll talk."

Her icy demeanor succeeded in chilling him to his core. It was generally acknowledged that if a woman said "fine", you were pretty much screwed.

She didn't leave him to wonder long. "The sheets on my bed are still warm from where we made love, yet you have the nerve to stand there and tell me Diane still holds a place in your heart?" Rage vibrated with the question she voiced.

"I didn't say that," he denied. "I didn't—in any way, shape, or form—say I love her. Don't put words in my mouth."

The flat of her hand shot out and caught him in his upper chest. "You're a damned liar," she snarled. "A two-timing sonofabitch!"

"Are you high? I just said I don't love her."

"You said she still means something to you," she shouted.

Muffled footsteps sounded from the hall. They'd have an audience soon enough.

Keaton tried to temper his own anger and plead his case. "Babe, you are being unreasonable. I only said..." He trailed off as the blackest of rages crossed her face. *Shit!* He used the word "unreasonable". How stupid could a guy be? "What I meant to say..." Backpedalling did no good now that the damage was done.

"Go home, Keaton."

"When you look back on this, you are going to see how wrong you are," he warned. "Don't do this to us again."

"I didn't do it to us the first time. You did that by slipping your dick into another woman."

"Autumn, you are letting your jealousy take root here. That ugliness will destroy everything."

"Let me clarify one thing. I'm not jealous of that skank. Not now, not ever. She isn't a pimple on my ass. But if you still want her, by all means, have at it."

"I don't want her!" he shouted. "I want you!"

The door flung open on his last words, and two of her sisters poured into the room.

"Hey, what's going on?" Spring was the first to speak after his shouted announcement.

"Damned if I know," he muttered and edged past her to exit the bathroom. "Ask your hot-headed sister."

He snatched up his shoes and shirt while the trio of women stood gaping at him. With one last, long look at Autumn, Keaton shook his head in disgust and exited the house.

"WHAT THE HELL WAS THAT ABOUT, TUMS?" WINNIE DEMANDED. "We heard you downstairs."

Autumn sagged back against the bathroom vanity and shook her head. She had no way of explaining how one little seed of doubt had blossomed into a large, hateful weed.

At the sound of Diane's name on Keaton's lips, she went insane. There was no other way to describe her behavior. He'd called her unreasonable, and he wasn't wrong. It was as if an alien being had invaded her body, caused massive destruction to her newfound relationship, then disappeared as quickly as it had come.

"I need a shower. I'll give you a rundown when I'm done, okay?"

They silently agreed and left her to her own devices.

As she lathered her skin, she replayed the morning in her mind. She couldn't come to grips with her meltdown. Sure, Diane was Autumn's trigger, but she knew Keaton came with baggage. Life was messy, and going forward with a relationship meant Autumn would have the past rear its nasty little head from time to time.

Bottom line, she owed him an apology.

She let the hot water pour over her face as she slowly spun in place. The feel of the water raining down on her skin soothed and centered her.

A quick sliver of charged air raced along her neck. It was all the warning she received before hands reached for her. Because she recognized the sensation, she guessed who her visitor was before she opened her eyes.

Looking up into Keaton's loving, apologetic blue gaze, the hurt faded.

"I'm sorry," they both said in stereo.

When he would've spoken again, she held up a hand. "You weren't the one in the wrong, Keaton. And I don't know what the hell came over me. For that, I'm sorry."

"I made it as far as my truck," he said huskily. "I couldn't leave it like that. Couldn't take the chance another misunderstanding would cost us years of our lives."

Wordlessly, she wrapped her arms around him and rested her cheek against his heart. "I was going to come to you after my shower. I don't want to fight."

"Good. Because neither do I." He lowered his head to hers and captured her mouth in a soul-searing kiss. The softness of his lips was in direct contrast with the aggressive action of his mouth. Keaton kissed like a man possessed. When they came up for air, he said, "I love you, Autumn. I know my actions in the past have been questionable, but I do love you with every fiber of my being." This time, he lightly brushed his lips across hers. "You are my reason for living. I never want to face another day without you."

"Damn, dude! You cornered the market on romantic apologies today."

"Yeah, I'm going to come up with my own line of I'm-Sorry-I-Fucked-Up greeting cards."

She laughed and kissed him more fully on the lips. "Let's finish and get Chloe. That is, if my bitchy self is still welcome at breakfast."

"You're always welcome—bitchy or no."

"Thank you for coming back."

He nodded and smoothed the soaked hair back from her face. "Are we okay?"

"I think so. There are a few things I still need to work through, but I'm willing to try."

"That's all I can ask, and it's more than I deserve."

"Like you said, you were young and stupid. I was too. But maybe we've got enough maturity between the two of us now that we can muddle through this thing called a relationship." She frowned when she finally noticed he was fully dressed. "You could've kicked off your shoes at least."

With a glance down and a sheepish grin, he shrugged. "All I thought was that I needed to get to you. I needed to touch you and tell you I love you one more time."

Her heart melted on the spot. How could it not?

Without breaking eye contact, she swirled her finger in the air to shut off the water.

"Impressive trick," he murmured.

"I love magic. Everything about it calls to me and fills me up. Maybe that's why I was devastated when you looked at me with such horror."

"You grew up with it. But me? Suddenly, the woman I loved had a ball of fire rotating on her palm. I almost crapped my pants."

She laughed and wrapped her arms around his neck. "I can see where it would be a bit intimidating."

"Can you? Because the knife in your hand and the wind bending the trees was downright terrifying. I was sure that at any minute, I'd wake up from some fucked-up dream. But each time I blinked, the unbelievable was still happening."

Autumn drew back marginally and studied his face. The truth of his statement was reflected there for her to see. "I'm sorry, Keaton. I never meant to terrify you. I realize now, it was a lot for you to absorb the way I revealed my gifts."

"You have nothing to be sorry for. No, I mean it," he said when she started to interrupt. "You expected me to be open-minded and not act like a child."

"Enough of this. We agreed the past is in the past." Palms out, she called the towels from the rack to her. She handed one to Keaton as she dried with the other. After she stepped out of the shower, she whirled her hands about her. A fresh pair of black jeans encased her ass nicely, while a brown shirt hugged her chest and showed it to its perfect advantage. A second wave of her hand perfected makeup and hair.

"You did in forty seconds what takes most women forty minutes," he laughed. "Impressive."

She grinned at him in the mirror and snapped her fingers to top the outfit with her favorite leather jacket. "Ready?"

"Think you could…?" He gestured to his wet clothing.

Another snap of her fingers sucked the moisture from his clothing and dried his outfit.

"Like I said, impressive."

She laughed and led the way from the room.

CHAPTER 18

The following days passed in a blissful haze for Autumn and Keaton. Every spare moment was spent together. Chloe was ecstatic about the change in their relationship. Diane was a non-issue in their happy little world since the day Alastair had put her in a trance. Autumn was afraid to rock the boat and avoided the topic of her ex-best friend. Keaton and Chloe seemed to be similarly inclined.

This morning, the three of them sat around the Carlyle kitchen island, eating the blueberry pancakes Keaton had whipped up.

"I forgot how good these were," Autumn moaned around her third bite.

A devilish light sparked his gaze as he studied her mouth. Without warning, he leaned forward to lick a maple syrup droplet from her bottom lip.

"Eww, Dad. Gross."

He turned wide-eyes on a disgusted Chloe. "What? I couldn't let her walk around all day with syrup on her lip."

With all the drama of an eight-year-old going on eighteen, Chloe rolled her eyes, making Autumn laugh.

"It is a bit unsanitary, isn't it?" she asked the girl, although secretly, she loved Keaton's attention.

Chloe nodded and shoveled in her own bite of pancake.

"You're going to have to get used to it, midget. It's the kind of corny, gross stuff adults do," Keaton told his daughter with a ruffle of her hair.

"Dad!" she cried and straightened the mess.

The two adults exchanged an amused glance. Chloe was fast approaching the age where appearances mattered. In just the few weeks since the pedicure party, she'd started wearing more girly clothes along with the lip gloss Autumn had purchased for her. It seemed it came along with pre-teen attitude. Today's discussion revolved around her desire to return to school.

"Why can't I go back?" Chloe asked for what felt like the millionth time.

Autumn decided to let Keaton field the question because explaining secrecy to a child was virtually impossible. They didn't understand the need to remain silent about witchcraft.

"I already said not yet, Chloe. This is not open for discussion."

The girl turned pleading eyes to Autumn. "Please. Tell him. He'll listen to you."

"I'm not going to get caught in the middle, kid. And it's not fair for you to try to shove me there." Autumn placed her fork on top of her plate and folded her arms in front of her on the table. With all her focus on Chloe, she said, "It's important to hide what we are. And while you feel you are grown up enough to handle the responsibility of remaining quiet on the subject, I'm here to tell you that you aren't."

"Why are you being mean?"

The tearful inquiry tugged at her heartstrings. "I'm not trying to be. You are no different from any witch or warlock who came before you. My sisters and I weren't allowed to go to school until we mastered our gifts and guaranteed we wouldn't talk about it to anyone."

"How old were you?"

"I was seventeen. Winnie was fifteen, and Summer was thirteen. Spring wasn't allowed to go to school until she was fourteen, her freshman year of high school."

"That's so old!" Chloe cried. "My friends will forget me."

"No they won't, midge," Keaton assured her.

The large honey-colored eyes filled with tears. "They will," she choked out. "And you don't care."

Chloe ran from the kitchen, leaving two helpless adults in her wake.

"I don't know what to do," he confessed.

"Perhaps you can talk to my dad. Maybe he can give you some pointers."

"I was terrified of your dad when I thought he was a mere mortal. Now that I know he is the second most powerful being on the planet, yeah, no."

"If he didn't kill you nine years ago, he's not likely to now," she teased.

He snagged a bite of her pancake. "Not inspiring confidence there, babe."

"Want me to go talk to her?"

"If you think you can help." Keaton sighed and set down his fork. "I only want what's best for her."

"I know." Autumn laid her hand over his. "On another note, Alastair is pressuring us for the stone. Are you any closer to deciding if you intend to relinquish it?"

"I know he says it's for your mom's benefit, but that guy is shady as fuck. What was that whole thing with Lin about? Those two hated each other. You and I were almost the victims of whatever feud they'd started."

"He did save us when he didn't have to. He could've waited for you to freeze to death and left me to burn."

"I know that too," he said with a sigh.

Autumn could sense his frustration. She could also feel the energy pulsing from the pendant hidden under his shirt. The pull toward the Chintamani Stone was unlike anything she'd ever experienced. Whenever she came in contact with it, she wanted it for her own.

Her head came up from where she'd been resting it on her hand. "Keaton?"

"Yeah?"

"When did Chloe start acting odd?"

He didn't deny his daughter's actions were off. "After the spa day. Why?"

"I think we need to get the stone away from her."

His dark brows shot almost to his hairline. "Pardon?"

"I don't think it's regular kid behavior. I can't be sure, but I think the necklace is influencing her moods."

With swift fingers, he unbuttoned his shirt to stare at the necklace. What he hoped to see, she had no idea.

"Maybe the stone isn't about granting wishes so much as it is about amplifying them. Or at least the emotions surrounding them," she suggested. "Why did I react badly to your comment about Diane the other day? Why is Chloe acting strange? She's a matter-of-fact kind of child. She doesn't throw tantrums."

He nodded slowly, staring intently at her.

Her heart sunk. She recognized that look.

Dollars to donuts, he believed his reaction to their love was too strong and perhaps enhanced by magic. *He intended to kick her to the curb.*

Vomit bottled up in the back of her throat, and she ran for the bathroom. As she deposited the contents of her stomach into the toilet, gentle hands pulled back her hair and caressed her neck.

"You okay, babe?"

With shaky hands, she ripped toilet paper off the roll and wiped the edges of her mouth. "I think so."

"I'll get your toothbrush, just sit here a second."

Why was he being so kind when he wanted her gone? What was wrong with her that she sat there like a pathetic blob, waiting for him to drop the axe? She should just go to Maine. Start a new life. Forget all things Keaton Carlyle.

As Autumn positioned herself to teleport, Keaton returned.

"Where are you going?"

"You only think you love me because of the stone. You—"

His hands came up to cup her face. "That's not you talking, babe. Think for a minute. What were you just saying about the Chintamani Stone messing with people?"

"But you…" She trailed off in confusion. "You don't believe the things you are feeling for me are related to the magic of the necklace?"

He smiled warmly. "No. I know I love you. If anything, I might worry you don't feel the same about me and that maybe you are being drawn in. But no, I know exactly how I feel."

"We have to get rid of that thing. Or, at the very least, store it in a safe place while we figure out if it's altering our moods. Although, you don't seem to be similarly affected like me and Chloe." Autumn ran the water and splashed out her mouth as she mentally ran through the reasons why the stone wouldn't alter Keaton's perspective of things. Was it because he was actually in possession of the thing? Because he was a male? She'd be curious to know if Knox and Cooper were experiencing any strange behavior. "Has there been anything off with your brother or Knox?"

"No, but then Knox has been in the barn with the new stock from sun up to sun down." A frown etched his forehead. "I can't recall anything specific, but I don't believe C.C. is acting odd."

"What is different about me and Chloe?"

They both registered the answer at the same time. "Physical contact," they said in unison.

"That makes the most sense," she said. "Chloe and you share hugs throughout the day. And as for us…" Heat rose in her cheeks.

He grinned. "Like rabbits."

"I know you don't want to, but I think this cements the decision to get rid of that thing."

The smile disappeared from his face. "No. It just means I shouldn't wear it."

"Keaton," she said warningly. "It's dangerous. Don't tell me you can't feel the power."

Irritation flared in his face. Then she knew—*Keaton was obsessed with the stone!*

She changed tactics. "You know what? I think you're right. My nervousness is probably a reaction to the necklace."

His brow cleared, and his smile returned.

"I'm going to pop home to clear my head of whatever the pull of this thing has. I'll call you later, okay?"

She didn't give him a chance to respond or touch her but instead teleported to Thorne Manor. When she arrived, she hit the ground running.

"Sisters!" she called with her mind and voice, sending the cry out to Summer at her Sanctuary in North Carolina. "I need you."

Within seconds, they were all gathered in the living room discussing the problem at hand.

"Keaton doesn't believe there's a problem. I think he's under the influence of that damned stone," Autumn said.

Her sisters all shared a speaking glance.

"What?"

Winnie was the first to answer. "What if you only gave Keaton a second chance because the pull of the stone?"

The thought hadn't occurred to her, but it should've. Nausea nearly caused her to lose her cookies for the second time.

"We don't know enough about this thing," Summer inserted. "We should call Alastair. He'll know what it does."

Spring spoke up with another option, "What about Nash?"

"My brother?" Summer shook her head. "I'm not sure bringing him into this is a good idea. He'll take it to the Witches' Council, and we'll never see the darned thing again. What if Alastair can't wake Mom without it?"

"Good point," Spring muttered and slouched back into her seat.

"Are we all in favor of calling Uncle Alastair?" Winnie asked.

Autumn took in the resolute expressions of her sisters. "I think so."

Summer picked up her smartphone and shot off a text. Before she could place it back on the table, there was a knock on the front door.

"Think it's him?" Spring whispered.

"Why are you whispering?" Autumn laughingly asked.

"He scares me," her sister admitted.

"Fair enough."

The knock sounded louder, and Autumn rose to her feet. "I'll get it."

She wasn't surprised to see her uncle on the other side of the door. But she *was* surprised to see him dressed casually in a pair of black slacks and a pale blue shirt. With his blond hair slightly mussed and the two-day growth of facial hair, the man looked as if he could be on the cover of GQ magazine.

"If I didn't already know round about your age, I'd never believe you were older than thirty-five," she said in real wonder.

His pleased grin had her lips twitching. Who knew old Uncle Alastair was susceptible to flattery?

His expression turned serious, and he gave her a visual once-over. "How are you feeling, child? Any lingering trauma or nightmares?"

The concern he conveyed rattled her. Unexpected tears clouded her vision. "I'm okay."

"You are the strongest woman I know, but if you need someone to talk to, I make a mean martini and am a great listener."

She surprised them both when she hugged him. "Thank you."

His arms tightened briefly before he released her. "Anytime."

Twenty minutes later, a course of action was agreed upon. Autumn would take the first opportunity to spirit away the Chintamani Stone and deliver it to Alastair, who would be on standby.

Keaton wouldn't be happy with her, but he'd given her no choice. That damned stone had to go for all their sakes.

"What will you do with it once you have it?" she asked her uncle.

"Certainly not wear it. Damned fool boy." Alastair shook his head. "His parents did him a disservice by not teaching him from birth."

"I tend to agree," Autumn said.

CHAPTER 19

*C*hloe sat on the park bench and toed the pebble at her feet. From the corner of her eye, she noticed a group of kids laughing and playing tag in the field that doubled for the local soccer practices. They were the same kids she used to ride bikes with, but who now ignored her and refused to allow her to play. The popular kids had kicked her out of their circle. Now she was friendless and bored.

Her anger at the unfairness boiled within her, and the wind picked up in intensity. When an older, black-haired man stopped in front of her, Chloe calmed the air around them.

While she was told never to talk to strangers, something about the man compelled her to speak. "Who are you?" she asked as she stared up into his pale green eyes.

"I'm a friend of your father, Chloe."

He smiled. The sight made butterflies dance in her stomach, but not in a good way like when cute Derek Sheehan was teasing her. *This* man's smile made her stomach hurt.

She sat frozen in place when everything inside her screamed at her to run.

Autumn was always saying to trust her instincts. But this man had the same look as her mother did when Mama was about to hit her. And like with Mama, Chloe knew it was better not to run. Running made her mother angrier.

His grip on her arm hurt where he rushed her toward the van.

From nowhere, Derek appeared in front of them, stopping the man from moving forward. "Where ye be takin' my friend?" The sound of his funny accent calmed some of Chloe's jumping nerves.

"Another witch. Why am I not surprised?" The mean man sneered.

Derek grinned, and his deep dimples flashed. He cast a quick look at Chloe and shot her a wink. "If ye know what I am, man, then ye know what I can do. Let Chloe go." Derek's voice, though hard with warning, was music to her ears. She loved his musical Irish manner of speaking. The steel behind his command shot him to hero status in her eyes.

"I don't have time for this," snarled the dark-haired man. "Seize him, too."

Men rushed Derek from the van opening behind him. But the young teen was faster and more wily than the attacking men. Derek teleported, reappearing behind her and the scary man.

"Run, Chloe. Run like the wind and don't be lookin' back," Derek whispered in her ear then struck down on the wrist of the arm clutching her tight.

The man's hold on her loosened. It allowed her to jerk away and run for all she was worth toward the police car pulling onto the road next to the park. "Uncle Coop!" she screamed with everything she had. "Uncle Coop!"

A gunshot echoed across the clearing. The screaming of her ex-schoolmates caused her to spin back. Derek crumpled to the ground at the dark-haired man's feet. His hands clutched to his stomach and mouth opened in a silent scream.

"Derek!" she cried. "Derek!"

She wanted to be brave and run toward him, but the scary man was now focused on her. Fear propelled her into motion, and she whirled to run. A line of people blocked her path, and for a moment, she panicked until a familiar voice called her name.

"Autumn?"

"I'm here, kid. Now this is what I want you to do. Listen carefully," Autumn said urgently. "You close your eyes and visualize Thorne Manor. Do you understand? I want you to smell the dirt, feel the breeze through the trees, picture the house. Can you do that?"

"Y-yes. But Derek—"

"I'll see to Derek, but first I need you safe. Now close your eyes and picture my home," Autumn ordered.

Chloe did as she was told. She blocked out everything else but what Autumn had said to imagine. When she opened her eyes, she was standing in front of the large three-story house.

"Miss Winnie!" she screamed. "Miss Winnie!"

Winnie, Spring, and Preston Thorne poured out of the house.

"Autumn... she's in trouble. A b-bad man tried t-to... D-Derek is hurt... I..." Sobs wracked her body and made an explanation impossible.

"Chloe," Spring stated her name calmly. "Sweetie, I need you to tell me where my sister is."

"P-park," she hiccuped out.

Winnie and Preston disappeared before another whimper could escape her.

"Uncle C-Coop, too," she added on a whisper.

"Good girl. Go inside our house. The house is warded and will not let anyone bad enter. Do you understand?"

She nodded, unable to speak.

"You're a brave girl, and when this is over, I want to hear about your first teleport," Spring said with a soft smile and a light caress of Chloe's cheek. "Run along now."

Chloe did what she was told and ran into the house. With the last of her courage, she bolted the door, and then huddled in the corner by the stairs to cry for Derek.

Autumn faced Lin and his four minions. "Picking on little girls now, you douche canoe?"

Hate burned from Lin's eerie pale-green eyes. "She was a means to an end. But now that you're here, I still have a pawn." He pointed his gun at her chest across the short distance.

"Let the Sheriff help the boy, and I'll go with you," she said. Where she found the courage, she'd never know. There was no doubt in her mind that if she went with him, she was as good as dead.

The left side of his lip curled. She was coming to hate that particular expression on his face. It always indicated an impending evil action on his part.

No one was prepared for the fog when it rolled in. Autumn hit the deck, dragging Coop down with her. The instinctive response saved her life as Lin's gun discharged.

The heavy gray mist didn't reach the ground but instead lingered about two feet above the grass and expanded upward. As Autumn army-crawled toward the writhing teen, she recognized the heeled boots heading for the fray.

Winnie.

If Autumn lived through this little showdown at the OK Corral, she intended to tell her sister how damned impressive this particular bit of magic was.

"Cloak," someone shouted.

Well, fuck! Why hadn't she thought of that?

Autumn silently mouthed the words to Granny Thorne's cloaking spell and threw her hands wide to encompass her sister, Coop, and Derek.

On hands and knees, she continued to crawl just in case the spell had gone awry.

When she reached Derek's side, his hopeless, pain-filled hazel eyes stared up at her, and a silent tear trailed down the side of the boy's face.

"You are not dying today," she whispered. "You hang on, do you hear me?"

He nodded and gripped the hand she held out.

In a flash, she had him in the living room of the Thorne estate.

"D-Derek?"

Chloe's tentative voice caught her attention.

"Chloe, come here, sweetheart. I need your help."

"I-I don't know w-what to do?"

"I'm going to show you, but I need you beside me."

The girl stayed huddled in the corner.

Autumn changed tactic. "Chloe, listen to me. Derek needs you. If you don't help me right now, he might die."

The harsh, no-nonsense tone penetrated the child's haze of fear and had her scrambling to Autumn's side.

"Remember how I taught you to harness your power? To feel it heat up within you and push out toward your fingers?"

"Yes."

"I need you to do that now. Lay your palms flat on Derek's stomach about three inches above his belly button." She took a precious few seconds to reposition Chloe's hands then went back to applying pressure to the wound. "Perfect. Don't pulse your power, push it. But instead of through your fingers, do it through the center of your palms. While you are doing that, I want you to visualize a white light. Got it?"

Chloe's dark head nodded.

"You do that until I tell you to stop."

"Okay."

With one hand, Autumn maintained pressure on the initial entry wound, while she dug out her cell-phone with the other. She placed one call to GiGi for help, and a second to Alastair to give him a ten-second rundown of the incident in the park.

He hung up after three. She could only assume he was going to wade into the fray.

GiGi showed as Autumn tossed the phone aside.

"Nice timing, Aunt GiGi."

"Move your hands and let me work."

Like the time a few months earlier when Summer had been shot, GiGi used the added boost of her wand and arched a magical purple light into the bullet hole. And as before, the healing light did its job. Within seconds the slug was removed, and the entrance wound was cauterized to stop the flow of blood.

Autumn knew there was more to it, but not being the healer of the family, she only grasped the basics.

"Is he going to be okay?" Chloe asked tearfully.

"He is, dear child. Thanks to you," GiGi said as she smoothed the girl's sweat-dampened hair back from her face. "You can let go now."

"What if he d-dies?" she whispered.

"He won't. Aunt GiGi is the best in the business. If she says Derek's going to be okay, then he's going to be just right as rain."

"He saved me from the b-bad man," Chloe said between sniffles.

"Then he's a true hero, child," GiGi informed her. "Now, go wash your hands and face, then wait in the kitchen for your father. Autumn and I are going to see young Derek is comfortable upstairs."

"Yes, Miss GiGi."

When Chloe was out of earshot, GiGi demanded the details.

Autumn told her what little she knew, including a rundown of her time at the monastery.

"Lin? You're sure his name was Lin?" GiGi asked sharply.

"Yes. Do you know him?"

"I do. As do Preston and Alastair. We all go back a long way."

"What's that fucker's deal? He's determined to see me burn at the stake."

"Lin was part of a task force to hunt witches and warlocks," GiGi informed her.

"Was? He isn't any more?"

The dark-blue eyes of her aunt—more serious than Autumn had ever witnessed them—took on a haunted look. "He's the only one left."

"Let me guess. He went up against Alastair and my father, and everyone on his side was wiped out."

"Yes."

"Goddess! No wonder he hates our family."

"He's the reason your mother is the way she is."

Autumn reeled with the news. "Lin is the reason Mom is in stasis?"

"For the most part, yes."

Wrapping her head around a story that had played out twenty years before was difficult. What was even more difficult was the thought that it had all come around again. Who would pay the price this time? Her? Keaton? Chloe?

Lin seemed to have a hard-on for making Autumn suffer. If she had to sacrifice herself to keep Chloe safe, she would. That little girl had come to mean more to Autumn than her own life.

"I need to check on Chloe. Can you teleport Derek to my old room?"

"Go. I will see to it. I will also let his parents know he will be in stasis here to finish healing."

"Thanks, Aunt GiGi. I love you."

"I love you, too, child."

Autumn found Chloe staring morosely at the table, her little hands folded in her lap as if she expected the worst sort of punishment.

"Hey, kid. You doing okay?"

The dark head came up, and tear-bright eyes blinked up at Autumn.

"Is he really going to b-be okay?"

"He really is," she assured the girl with a hug. "Thanks in huge part to you. Your magic helped me to keep him stable until GiGi could work on him. You should be super proud of yourself. I know *I'm* proud of you."

"It's my f-fault," Chloe said tearfully as she swiped her running nose with the back of her sleeve.

Autumn conjured a box of tissues and set it on the table. Next, she conjured a three-tiered chocolate cake with chocolate butter-cream frosting, two plates, and a couple of forks. "How so?"

"If I hadn't g-gone with that man, Derek wouldn't have t-tried to save me. He wouldn't have been h-hurt." Chloe's words were peppered with little catches from her emotional upset.

Autumn squatted next to the child and brushed a hand along her hair. "You can't think like that. Derek chose to help you of his own free will. And I'm sure he doesn't regret a second of saving you, because that's what he did." She kissed Chloe's forehead. "Lin is a very bad man who is out to hurt my family. He was going to use you to get to me because I love you. If anyone is to blame, it's me."

The air crackled around them, signaling a group teleport. Autumn's sisters, along with her dad, Coop, and Keaton all appeared in the hallway off the kitchen. Coop and Keaton looked a little haggard, but her sisters and father looked as if they'd been for a stroll instead of in a fight for their lives.

Keaton was the first to reach Autumn and Chloe. He hauled his daughter into his arms and held on tight.

"I'm sorry, Daddy," she sobbed. "I'm sorry."

"Don't you dare apologize. You did nothing wrong," he returned gruffly.

Tears burned behind Autumn's lids as she watched the scene unfold. Keaton was the best of fathers.

Still holding Chloe, Keaton reached up and jerked the necklace from where it was anchored around his neck. With a show of disgust, he threw it on the table in front of Autumn. "I'm out of this whole crazy mess. Do what you want with that, I don't care. But when it affects my daughter..." He compressed his lips, unable to finish.

Autumn reached for his arm, but he backed away. "Keaton?"

He shook his head and backed from the room with Chloe clinging tightly to his neck, her spindly legs wrapped around his waist. "I'll call you tomorrow."

The ugly, negative feelings seizing her chest weren't pleasant. She wouldn't hold her breath for that call. With shaky fingers, she lifted the necklace and slipped it into her pocket. The damned thing had to be cursed, but she intended to follow through and deliver it to Alastair. It was long past time to get it out of their lives and in a more secure location.

CHAPTER 20

$\mathcal{K}$ eaton's phone call came an hour later. Without preamble, he asked, "How do I ward my home?"

"You can check with your parents to see if perhaps they've already done it. But it isn't difficult. Your family grimoire should have a recording of the process."

"Can Chloe be safeguarded against danger with a spell?"

She grimaced at the aggressive tone in his voice. While she understood it, she needed to tread carefully. Keaton was on the edge, and any little thing could set him off.

"Not that I know of, but I can come over and help you research—"

"No. Your family has done enough," he snapped.

"Keaton—"

"I don't want to talk about this now. I have a terrified daughter who is devastated because her friend was shot on her behalf. I can't deal with your family drama right now, Autumn."

His attitude was warranted, but it hurt nonetheless.

"Let Chloe know that Derek will wake in a few days' time. If she wants to visit him at any point, she is more than welcome."

"She can wait until he wakes and visits her here. I don't want her anywhere around any of you until the threat of Lin is neutralized."

"Understood."

Keaton hung up without a by-your-leave or even a fuck you. His coldness was reminiscent of their fight in the clearing all those years ago. The ache it caused her heart was debilitating.

"That the boyfriend?"

She spun around and faced her father. "I don't know if he'd consider himself my boyfriend at this point. Putting his kid in danger might've been the deal-breaker."

"He'll come around."

"I don't know, Dad," she said as she sat at the kitchen table. To avoid his penetrating gaze, she picked at the cake frosting. "He's pretty pissed—and rightfully so."

"He'll realize this was not your fault," Preston assured her.

"But it is my fault. If I hadn't agreed to go after the Chintamani Stone for Uncle Alastair, I wouldn't have put Keaton and Chloe on Lin's radar."

"We've always been on his radar, child. His brand of hatred goes back centuries."

She frowned as her father settled across from her and cut a slice of cake for them both. "How can he be that old?"

"He isn't, but the society he worked for was. It was known as the Désorceler Society. For generations, it was his family's job to hand select the members to hunt witches and warlocks." Preston shrugged and chewed a bite of cake before continuing. "When the Witches' Council decided on a counter attack, a large-scale battle ensued. Lin's entire family were casualties of the war. Mother and younger brother included."

"Oh, Dad!" While she hated Lin, she felt compassion for what he'd been through. "Aunt GiGi said Lin was responsible for Mom's stasis state. Was it part of that war?"

Preston sighed and laid down his fork. "Yes and no. The war took place about twenty years before you were born." His dark amber eyes looked through her, at some distant memory. A minute or two ticked by before he explained. "Your mother and my brother Alastair had been childhood sweethearts. They were inseparable. Like you and your Keaton in the early days when you first dated."

Autumn nodded her understanding.

He picked up his fork and toyed with the layers of the cake. "I loved her even then. Her laughter. Her flashing eyes. I knew she loved Alastair, but I didn't care. In my heart, I wanted her for myself.

"Then the Witches' Council called my brother to fight. I was only sixteen at the time, but powerful in my own right. Not nearly as powerful as Alastair or my father, but strong. Or so I thought. I was naive."

She covered one of her father's large hands where it rested on the table, but remained silent.

Preston flipped his hand and entwined their fingers. "Warlocks are notoriously hard to kill, but it isn't impossible. There were traitors out to save their own hides. The Désorcelers were far-reaching. They made promises they had no intention of keeping, but those witches or warlocks in fear for their own lives had no way of knowing that."

"What happened?" Autumn asked softly. "How did you and Mom end up married?"

"Alastair was captured. Rumor came to us that he'd been tortured and killed. I lived for years with the belief that it had been all my fault. Had I not been there that day, he would never have been taken. But he sacrificed himself for me. For his little brother."

"Oh, Dad."

"Aurora continued to mourn him for years. In the beginning, she was inconsolable. She told me later, she felt her only recourse was to leave Leiper's Fork. One day, years later, I came across her while traveling. I think perhaps we were both trying to run from the pain of loss."

"Where did you meet?"

"France. A little out-of-the-way village. There she was, sitting at an outdoor cafe, reading a book, and sipping coffee." He smiled at the memory. "I couldn't believe my eyes. Anyway, we struck up a conversation, and the rest was history. We grew close and married, had you kids. Then three years into our marriage, Alastair showed up —alive and well. Or as well as someone who had been held captive for years could be."

"She left with him?"

Preston shook his head. "Not at first. But at night, when she thought I wasn't listening, I could hear her crying. I didn't doubt that she loved me. But it was never going to be a fraction of the love she held for my brother."

"I'm sorry, Dad," she whispered around the lump in her throat.

He patted her hand and conjured a brandy. After a fortifying sip, he continued. "You know about the affair and the birth of your twin sisters."

"I do."

"I hated him at that point. Hated her too. But I didn't feel as if I could live without her. So I clung with all my might—to her, to the twins. Except Holly had an aversion to me. I don't know why. For as much as Summer loved being in my arms, Holly was the complete opposite. If I came near, she'd scream."

He took another long drink. "Aurora decided to send Holly to Alastair. And afterward, your mother was a shell of her old self. She was so unhappy. One day, I came home, and she was gone. No note. No goodbye." He used the heel of his hands to rub his eyes. "I knew she'd gone to him. But at least she left me you kids. It gave me something to live for."

"How did she end up in stasis?" Winnie asked from behind Autumn, startling both her and Preston.

"Lin caught up with them. His intent was to kill my brother, but Aurora moved in the path of the bullet. It tore through her chest and nicked an artery. A wound like that can be healed if a witch is quick enough. But the bullets he uses are laced with a special poison. One deadly to witches. GiGi and Alastair were sick for days after they attempted to heal her."

"What?" Surely Autumn had misheard.

Preston froze in sipping his drink.

"Dad, Chloe helped me and GiGi heal Derek!"

He shoved to his feet and grabbed Autumn's hand. "Winnie, get GiGi and tell her to head to the Carlyle estate." With that, he teleported himself and Autumn to Keaton's house.

"Keaton!" she screamed as soon as she saw him sitting on the porch swing. "Chloe! We have to get to Chloe!"

Keaton surged to his feet and didn't stop moving until he hit Chloe's bedroom. Preston and Autumn were hot on his heels.

They all skidded to a halt when they saw the child lying on the floor by her dolls. Sweat beaded the little girl's brow, and her pain-filled eyes stared straight ahead.

"Good Christ!" Keaton shot to his knees and cradled her close. "She's barely breathing!"

"Move aside," Preston ordered.

"No! I—"

Autumn fisted a hand and jerked sideways. Keaton's arms dropped down, allowing Preston to scoop up Chloe before she hit the floor. Because the rage in his eyes promised retribution, she fisted her other hand to keep Keaton frozen in place.

"Take her into the living room, Dad. GiGi should be here any second."

An inhuman cry erupted from Keaton, and he shifted in place. Her hold on him was weakening fast. In about one minute, she was going to be dealing with over six-feet of enraged male.

"Keaton, you need to calm down. You are not helping Chloe. She needs the help only my father and GiGi can provide," she said, trying to infuse a calm note to her voice.

He snarled his response.

"Keaton, please," she pleaded. Sweat broke out on her own upper lip. Whatever Lin had laced those bullets with was now coursing through her own veins. She'd been poisoned along with Chloe, but she refused to draw attention to herself until the child was cared for. "Let them help her."

Once again, he shifted. Her fragile hold broke. He shoved by her and charged from the room. Knowing she'd done all she could, she used the last of her magic to teleport home. She never made it farther than the foyer before she collapsed in a heap on the old oak floors.

"You do know Autumn was poisoned too, brother."

Keaton rounded the corner to the living room and overheard GiGi's comment.

"I know. She wants us to treat Chloe first." Preston's response was gruff.

"There may not be enough to treat Chloe, Autumn, and the boy," GiGi warned as she injected the syringe tip into Chloe's vein.

"What are you doing?" Keaton demanded. "What did you give her?"

"Calm down, son," Preston growled. "It's an antidote to the poison Lin used."

"Lin?" Keaton's gaze ping-ponged between Preston and GiGi. "Lin poisoned my daughter?"

"The bullet was laced with poison that is fatal to witches. When Chloe and Autumn helped Derek, they were infected," GiGi explained.

"Why weren't you?" he asked as he rushed to his daughter's side. "Or me, for that matter?"

"Because I didn't use direct magic on Derek. I used a tool. Chloe and Autumn were hands on."

Panic swelled in his chest, and Keaton had a hard time grasping what was being said. His daughter had been lying in her bedroom —dying—as he sat brooding on the porch and nursing a beer.

He knelt beside her and brushed the dark hair back from her pale face. "When will we know?"

"Twenty-four hours," GiGi said as she packed up her small bag of medicines. She handed him a slip of paper with her phone number. "Keep pushing liquids and call me if anything changes in her condition. Where's Autumn?"

He frowned and looked toward the hall. She should've arrived right behind him. "I left her in the bedroom."

Preston ran for the room and came back alone. "She must've headed back to the manor." To Keaton, he said, "Don't be an ass this time around, son. She was only trying to help you and yours."

"She's the reason my daughter is in this condition," Keaton snapped.

Autumn's father shook his head with a look of pity. "From one stubborn fool to another, don't let pride be your downfall," he said and disappeared.

"My brother isn't wrong. Lin and his kind would've found your family eventually. It's what he does." GiGi patted the shoulder closest to her. "Get your parents back here immediately to help extend the perimeter and enforce the wards on your estate. Phillip will know how it's done," she said, referring to his father. "Call me if Chloe worsens."

Then she, too, was gone. Keaton was left alone with his suffering child and a purple card that contained a single phone number.

In the long hours during the night, he kept vigil beside his daughter's bed. Knox and C.C. took turns delivering soup, coffee, and fresh water for him to bathe Chloe. By morning, his parents had returned, thanks to Coop's summons.

"How is she?" Phillip asked.

"No change," Keaton answered without emotion. He was too spent.

"You should get some rest. I can sit with her for a while," his mother offered.

"I can't leave her, Mom. I just can't."

The smell of her subtle perfume surrounded him just before her arms embraced him. "Let me know what I can do."

"Can you check on Autumn?" he asked hoarsely, all the worry for her in his voice. Now that he'd calmed down and had a chance to think things through, he realized none of this was her fault. GiGi had been correct; Lin would've found them regardless. "She... she might not..."

"Consider it done, son," his father said.

CHAPTER 21

*A*utumn wandered aimlessly along the river's edge, surprised by how mild the weather seemed. They were only a few months away from winter, yet flowers still bloomed along the riverbank and birds sang their happy songs as they swooped from tree branch to tree branch.

She smiled at the beauty of the day. If only every day were this lovely.

After another few minutes of walking, she encountered a solitary figure on a bench overlooking the water. The woman's soft smile widened, and her stunning eyes burned with love.

"Hello, dear one."

"Hello."

Who exactly the female was, Autumn didn't know, but the peace she experienced in the other woman's presence was immeasurable.

Autumn studied her for a moment, taking in the long, shining black hair, the kohl-lined, light amber eyes, and the smooth, olive complexion. The woman wore a sheer, white dress with a material that reflected just enough light to provide modest coverage of her ample assets. The dress draped over her left shoulder, held together with a jeweled clasp. A gold scorpion bangle balanced the look and graced her upper right arm. In her hand, she held a long staff with a dark yellow stone at the tip.

"Do I know you?" Autumn asked as she shifted forward.

"You do." The amusement in the other woman's voice was thick.

"Who are you?"

"Isis."

"Isis? As in the Goddess Isis?"

"Yes."

"Huh." It was probably bad form, but Autumn plunked down on the bench beside where the Goddess stood. Seeing your ancestor mysteriously appear during your morning walk had that effect.

Isis's full red lips twitched in amusement. "Do you know why you are here, dear?"

Autumn frowned and looked around. She turned confused eyes to the Goddess. "No. I... Where am I?"

"You know it as the Otherworld," Isis said gently and paused to allow her words to sink in.

Dear Goddess! She was dead. That was the only reason to be in the Otherworld.

It took three tries before Autumn could speak, but she finally managed to croak, "I'm dead?"

"Nearly."

"I didn't get to say goodbye," she cried.

"There was no time. Come. There is someone I'd like you to meet."

Autumn followed Isis to a clearing that was eerily similar to the one between the Thorne and Carlyle estates. "Is this...?"

"Yes. Just on a different plane of existence."

"Gotcha." She choked back the million questions dancing about in her mind.

They stopped on the exact spot where Autumn and Keaton had fought nearly ten years before.

"Why are we here?" she asked.

"Patience. She will be here soon."

"She?"

"Chloe."

"No!" Autumn yelled. "No! You don't get to take her. She's inno-cent." Tears, once they started, refused to stop flowing from her eyes. "Please!"

Isis cupped Autumn's cheek and ran a thumb under her eyes to dry the moisture there. "The decision is not mine. Nor is it yours. The decision to stay or go belongs to young Chloe alone."

"You don't understand. Keaton can't lose her. He won't be able to survive the loss."

"This is not about Keaton's journey, dear one. This is about Chloe's journey."

"Please!" she begged.

"You and your young man share a great love. If your daughter should decide to stay, you will get through this together."

"Our daughter?" Autumn's hand rested against her abdomen. "But our daughter died before she was born."

"No. The physical body died. Her spirit remained and took the form of another," Isis corrected.

"Chloe would've been my daughter?" Autumn asked incred-ulously.

"Yes. Your souls have been tied together for many incarnations."

Knees weak, Autumn leaned against a nearby tree. "My daugh-ter? Chloe was mine first?"

Isis didn't answer; she merely smiled.

The sun flared brighter as the little girl stepped into the clearing.

"Autumn!" Chloe yelled happily as she ran across the glen.

They met halfway in a tangle of arms. "Oh, Chloe," she cried softly.

"Did she tell you? Did Isis tell you that you are my mom?" the girl asked unable to contain her excitement.

"She did, sweetie."

"Isn't that the best thing ever?"

"It is."

Tears poured unchecked down Autumn's face.

Chloe pulled back with a frown. "Why are you crying? Aren't you happy?"

"Sometimes adults cry when they are overwhelmed with happiness," she said on a husky whisper. It was all she could manage past the thick lump in her throat.

The girl turned her shining gaze upon Autumn.

How had she missed the similarity in the color and shape of their eyes? *A witch's tell.*

"I love you, kid. You know that, right?"

"I love you, too, Autumn."

"Apparently, you need to make a decision about returning to your dad."

"I know." Chloe grew quiet for a moment and looked back over her shoulder toward the Carlyle estate. "Derek is here, too."

Autumn's inquiring gaze sought Isis. A slight nod confirmed Chloe's pronouncement.

"Seems the three of us ended up in a pickle, huh?" she tried to joke.

"It's okay. We like it here."

"But your dad will be sad without you, Chloe. Derek's parents will be as well."

Isis joined them and placed one hand on each of their shoulders. "Two must go, one must stay. You must decide soon. Balance must be kept in all things."

"I'll stay," Autumn stated decisively. "The children return to live out their lives."

"No!" Chloe started to cry. "I don't want to go without you."

Autumn squatted in front of the girl and gripped her hands. "You'll have your dad and Derek. And my sisters will still be around to spoil you rotten."

"Not without you," Chloe cried.

"Chloe, I need you to be brave. You have a full life of beautiful things ahead." Autumn looked to the Goddess for confirmation. When Isis bestowed a single nod, Autumn addressed the child.

"Besides, you're the president of our Witch Club, remember? Who's going to keep my sisters in line?"

"B-but I l-love you," Chloe whispered brokenly.

No longer able to hold back, Autumn clutched Chloe to her. "I'm sorry. I'm sorry I won't be there to watch you grow up. But your dad will be, and he's going to love you enough for both of us."

Together they rocked, back and forth, holding each other in their last goodbyes.

"It is time," Isis said.

"I love you, Chloe. You hold tight to that and remember it always, okay?"

The girl nodded once, grabbed onto Isis's outstretched hand, and then was gone.

Left alone in the clearing, she collapsed onto the cool grass and stared up at the canopy of branches overhead. Hard to believe her heart could feel the weight of a thousand bricks in the Otherworld, but it did. It beat hard and heavy in her chest. Would she ever associate this stupid clearing with anything but loss?

Time passed, the only indication was the sun shifting positions in the sky.

Isis returned. "It is done."

"Chloe and Derek are going to be okay?"

"Yes."

Autumn nodded and continued to stare skyward. "What happens to me now?"

"There is someone else you need to meet."

"Please don't tell me it's someone else I love. I can't go through this again," she rasped out.

"Come, dear one."

THE SMALL HAND CRADLED WITHIN KEATON'S SPASMED AND WOKE him from his half-dosing state.

"Chloe? Baby?"

"Daddy?" she whispered

"Welcome back, sweetheart."

"Autumn is gone."

He leaned forward, unsure if he heard correctly. "What?"

"She was supposed to be my mom, but now she's gone."

Heart hammering, he smoothed a hand across her cheek. "That's just your fever talking. I'm sure Autumn is fine."

"She's not. She stayed with the Goddess," Chloe tearfully insisted.

Keaton's body turned cold, then hot. There was a truth in the solemn amber eyes staring up at him. He shook his head back and forth in denial. Autumn was too alive. Too vital. There was no way she was dead.

She wouldn't leave him. She'd fight like hell to stay. Wouldn't she?

Not if she believed you didn't care one way or another.

Hot tears burned his eyes and blurred his vision. Preston Thorne had been right to call him a fool.

"How are you feeling?" he choked out.

With solemn eyes, she studied his face. "Will you go check on her, Daddy?"

"I can't leave you, midget."

"Yes, you can. Derek and I both came back. Autumn made me. She also said to keep everyone in line."

Again, he shook his head in denial. The words sounded as if Chloe honestly believed what she was saying. The terrifying part was that Autumn really *would* cross the planes of existence to save the children. Was that what she had done? Used magic to save them and became trapped?

"You said the Goddess. What Goddess?" he asked, desperate for her to be wrong and this to be a made-up dream.

"Isis."

Isis! C.C. had recently mentioned the Thornes were descended from Isis.

He whipped out his phone, but just as he intended to dial her number, his phone rang.

"Winnie? What's going on?" he demanded hoarsely.

"Keaton? It's Autumn. She's…" A hiccuping sob escaped her. "We thought, if Chloe was out of the woods, you might want to come." The rest of her words were muffled by her crying, but they sounded a lot like "last goodbyes."

His eyes locked with Chloe's sad gaze. *She knew!*

He nodded, kissed her forehead, and ran for the door. "Mom!"

His mother was there in a second.

"It's Autumn, I have to go. Can you—?"

"Go. I'll stay with Chloe."

"She's awake. Just now. She may be hungry."

"Keaton, go!"

He raced out of the house and to the nearest vehicle, not caring who owned it. Luckily, with the exception of Coop's police cruiser, everyone usually left their keys in the ignition.

In mere minutes, he'd pulled into the driveway of Thorne Manor. Spring was outside wrapped in her father's embrace. Her devastated expression told the story.

"Is she…?" Keaton couldn't voice his worst fear.

Preston viewed him with red-rimmed eyes. "She's fading fast, son. You should go in."

He wasn't sure how he managed the stairs as quickly as he did, but in an instant, he was by Autumn's bedside. Winnie touched his shoulder and exited the room.

Autumn's skin was light gray, and her hair hung in lank strands across her shoulders. Her breathing was so shallow as to not be existent. She looked as if death had already taken her into its embrace.

"Oh, babe," he whispered. "No. Please, no."

No movement or response of any kind came from her.

"This isn't how we end. You don't get to die on me."

Silence.

"If you go, you'll take a piece of me that can never be replaced."

A sob caught in his throat. "Do you want that on your eternal conscience? Me, alone the rest of my days, with no one to love?"

Continued silence. He'd never seen her so motionless.

Keaton raised his head to stare upward at the ceiling. He wasn't sure what he intended until the words poured forth. "Isis? Goddess, if you can hear me, I'm begging you..." he paused to draw in a ragged breath. "...don't take her from me. Whatever I have to do, I'll do. You want my life? It's yours. Just bring her back." The sobs shook him, and his grief poured out in his words. "Please bring her back. Please. I love her. Please."

Because he needed the contact, needed to hold her one last time —if only in some small way—he wrapped his arms around Autumn's stomach and rested his cheek against her flat abdomen. "Please," he begged on a whisper.

Shadows filled the room, and Autumn's family came and went. The current mood was somber while everyone was on death watch, expecting her to breathe her last breath at any moment. Still, he continued to hold her, afraid if he let go, so would she.

At one point, young Derek entered the room, looking healthy but a little pale. "She saved me."

"And you saved Chloe." Keaton's voice sounded gravelly, even to his own ears. "Thank you."

The young teen stroked a finger down Autumn's gray cheek. "She told me to tell you there is a way."

Keaton's head swiveled to stare. "Who? Who told you? Autumn? How?"

"Isis. She told me to tell you there is still a way."

Heart kicking back into gear, Keaton rose to his feet. "What do I have to do?"

"She said, 'Alastair will know.'"

Keaton grabbed the boy by the shoulders and gave him a light shake before he hauled him close for a bear hug.

"Mr. Carlyle, you're hurting me, sir."

"Yeah, sorry about that, kid. I just..." He swallowed audibly and tried again. "I can't thank you enough."

"She also said that you only have until sunrise. Balance must be kept in all things."

"Stay with her. With Autumn. Talk to her. Let her know I'm coming back for her."

"Yes, sir."

CHAPTER 22

*K*eaton flew down the stairs and found the man he was looking for in the kitchen. "Mr. Thorne, there's a way to save her."

Preston frowned his disbelief. "Son, I think grief has sent you over the edge."

"No. Let me explain." He told Preston about his conversation, first with Chloe, then with Derek. "They both said virtually the same thing."

"Children's imaginations."

"I might've thought that too if they'd been awake and together these last days. But they haven't. Not even a phone conversation. And Derek isn't a young child prone to imagination."

"You're asking the impossible, Keaton. My brother wouldn't help me in a million years."

"But he might help Autumn. He has before. Would it hurt to ask? We can give him what he wants most—the Chintamani Stone."

The reality of what they held hit both men at once. "The stone!"

"That has to be what Isis was referring to. I'd wager only Alastair knows how to use it," Keaton said. "How do we contact him?

"The stone is scheduled to be turned over to the Witches' Council tomorrow morning," Preston warned.

"That's fine by me because we only have until dawn according to Derek."

"I'll summon him," Preston agreed wearily.

The two men were headed to the stairs when a pounding started on the large Mahogany entry doors. Preston reached the door first.

On the other side, Alastair, resplendent in a blue suit and pale yellow silk tie, leaned against the door jamb with his arms crossed over his chest. "You rang?"

"How did you...? How did he...?" Keaton was at a loss. If he lived to be two thousand years old, he'd never get used to how casually these men navigated the magical world.

Preston and Alastair stared at each other in challenge. Neither man giving an inch.

"Oh, for fuck's sake!" Keaton snapped. "Alastair, we need your help. Autumn has very little time left, and the Goddess Isis claims you're the key to saving her."

Alastair straightened and became all business. "Where is she?"

"Follow me," Preston commanded.

"My understanding was that she wasn't shot. How did this happen?" Alastair lifted her lids, checked her pulse, and placed an ear to her chest to listen for respiratory sounds.

"She saved me, sir," Derek said from his corner of the room. "I was shot by the man trying to take Chloe."

"The bullet was laced with a poison from Lin," Preston added.

Grimness settled over Alastair's features. "At this point, her chances are slim. You understand that, right?" He looked directly at his brother. "I don't know how much I can do."

"I know," Preston said gruffly. "Please, try."

"You know I will. Where's the stone?"

Suspicion clouded Preston's countenance.

"Brother, I need it to heal her. *The stone.*"

In a snap, Preston was dangling the necklace from his balled-up fist. When Alastair reached for it, Preston jerked it back. "When you're done, I have to turn it in to the Council."

Alastair raised an angry brow but remained silent.

Preston dumped the necklace in his brother's open palm. "But if I forget and set it on the kitchen table, say, while I run to check on my daughter, and if the necklace disappears, who can blame me for the distraction?"

Wicked amusement lightened Alastair's sapphire gaze. "Not a soul." He studied Preston's face before he spoke again. "We need one more thing."

"GiGi." It wasn't a question, but a statement. Preston shook his head. "She won't be in the same house as you, brother."

"Not even for Autumn?" Keaton asked, appalled at the idea anyone would put an old argument above the life of a loved one.

The brothers shared another speaking glance, and Keaton was left to wonder what the hell had gone on in this damned family. Right now, he didn't care as long as they put aside their differences long enough to save the woman he loved.

"What about Nash?" Preston referred to Alastair's estranged son.

"It's a possibility. I know he has the book smarts. But I don't know if he's practiced physically healing anyone." Alastair pulled his smartphone from his coat pocket and made the call.

A young man, nearly the spitting image of Alastair, arrived within minutes. Three massive ancient tomes were cradled in his arms. "Table," he commanded.

Preston was quick to fulfill the request. As Nash spread the books out on the flat surface, he discussed various poisons and how they affected the nervous system of a witch. "The key would be to isolate the toxin used."

"GiGi indicated it might be a mixture of Wolfsbane and Witchbane laced with arsenic," Preston volunteered.

Keaton's eyes widened. Even he knew Wolfsbane and arsenic were poisonous. He wondered at the Witchbane. As a newbie to the world of magic, he had no clue what that particular herb could do.

"Thank you for coming, son," Alastair said to Nash.

"I didn't do it for you," Nash said coldly. "I'm doing it for Autumn. Though why I would help a woman who punched me in the face is beyond me."

A burst of inappropriate laughter escaped Keaton. All eyes turned to him, and he shrugged. "Sorry. It sounds like something she'd do." To Nash, he said, "If it makes you feel any better, she nailed me in the gut a few weeks back. She has a wicked right."

Nash's lips twitched, and his eyes drifted to the woman on the bed. "It's appropriate that she's a fire element." He turned serious once again. "Let's get to work."

"What's first?" Keaton wanted to know.

Nash held out his empty hand. A moment later, a needle and four tubes appeared. "We draw her blood and test it."

When Nash moved to insert the tip into Autumn's vein, Alastair stopped him with a hand on his forearm. "Gloves. Whatever this poison is, it's extremely toxic. You prick her and then accidentally prick yourself, we'll have two of you in stasis."

Nash gave a short nod and conjured a pair of gloves for his hands. "Better?"

Alastair backed away to give Nash the space he needed to work. "GiGi used to have an antidote."

"She used the last of it on Chloe yesterday," Preston volunteered from where he rested his back against the wall. "She couldn't make more because the herb used to counteract the poison is now extinct."

Fear crawled about in Keaton's chest and restricted his ability to breathe. If they didn't have what they needed, what were Autumn's chances of survival?

Even as he thought it, he noticed a small potted plant appear on the table that hadn't been there moments before. "Uh, guys." When the Thorne men shot him curious stares, he pointed. "Is that the herb?"

"How the hell did you conjure that?" Alastair demanded.

"I didn't. It appeared."

"A gift from the Goddess," Derek explained.

Keaton approached the teen. "Do you have a direct connect to her right now? How do you know that?"

"I've been receiving messages from her since I woke up," the boy explained.

Hope bloomed, and Keaton grinned. "She wants us to save Autumn."

Derek nodded and offered a tentative smile.

"Where does the balance come in? You mentioned that earlier."

"It's a cosmic balance," Nash inserted into the conversation. "I've read about it. If Isis is offering to save Autumn, she wants something in return."

"Something or someone?" Keaton demanded. "Autumn wouldn't want anyone to take her place."

"The text wasn't exactly clear on the scroll I acquired." Nash gave a very Autumn-like shrug. "But it indicated an exchange was needed."

Keaton returned his attention to Derek. "Does she say which?"

The boy shook his head.

"Let's not look beyond the gift Isis is trying to provide," Alastair advised. "We don't have time to examine her motives if we want to save Autumn before dawn."

As Alastair placed the necklace around Autumn's neck, Keaton couldn't help but think her color shifted to a slightly lesser shade of gray.

Preston said as much.

"It's the stone," Alastair informed them. "It has a life-restoring force."

"But how? It alters the moods of those around it," Keaton protested.

Alastair's gaze sharpened on him. "You continued to wear it after we returned?"

"For about a week."

"Foolish boy. You didn't know the power you possessed. One wrong slip of the tongue..." Alastair's anger was a sight to behold.

The rage simmered below the surface, and his eyes blackened to coal. Terrifying to the extreme.

"I didn't know," Keaton said lamely.

"Damned novice," Alastair muttered.

"Cut him a break. Not everyone is as all-knowing as you," Nash said.

"I called you, didn't I?" Alastair snapped. "Obviously, I believe you are the most knowledgeable person to consult."

Preston pushed off the wall. "Let's shelve the animosity and help my daughter, please."

"What needs to be done with the plant?" Keaton ventured. "I can get started on that."

"Actually, you can wake Winnie and see what she has in her workshop to extract what is needed from the plant," Alastair suggested. He faced his brother. "Try to get GiGi here. She's the most skilled healer of us all." To Derek, he said, "Wake my niece Spring. With her skills, she might be able to graph a section and grow more plants. I don't want to destroy the last plant in existence."

"And Summer?" Preston asked.

"I don't think there is much she can do right now other than lend support. Let her sleep." He ran a hand through his hair, mussing it. "I need to bounce back to my home for magical supplies. Nash, can you create a list?"

"I'll go with you. There may be useful items I can't think of off the top of my head."

"Shouldn't someone stay with her?" Keaton was loath to leave her alone.

"I'll stay until you return, son. Hurry and wake Winnie."

Alastair's small kindness threw him. The man was hard as steel, and yet, on occasion, he actually seemed compassionate and downright human. The turnabout kept Keaton rattled. Most likely, that's what Alastair intended.

When Keaton returned to Autumn's room with Winnie, Alastair nodded and teleported with Nash. It gave Keaton time to wrap his mind around the consequences should their last-ditch effort to revive Autumn fail.

"I love you," he said huskily as he stared down into her beautiful, still face. "You fight from your side to return, and we'll fight like hell from this side to bring you back, okay?" He traced the outline of her features. "Tell Isis, I want you back, and if I can't have you here with me, I want to go with you into the afterlife."

The air shimmered in response to his words. An image of the glen flashed before it was gone again.

His gaze shot to a startled Winnie. "What the hell was that?"

"I don't know. I've never seen anything like that before."

"I could swear it was the clearing between our houses."

Her face lit with hope. "Of course! We have to get her to the clearing!"

"I don't understand."

"You will when you see it."

Winnie's sense of excitement was contagious.

"Okay, how do we transport her. Do we wait for the others to return?"

"Yes. Let me run to the attic and get what I need." She tossed him a set of gardening shears. "Clip off a piece of that plant. Not from the top. A leaf with a partial stem should do it." She paused on her way out the door. "Better multiply that by three just in case."

When she was gone, he approached the herb which resembled a basil plant. How could something as small as this provide what they needed it to?

The others returned, and within minutes, they'd moved their entire healing operation to the clearing. They formed a circle of the people present. Derek, who was still weak from his ordeal, watched from outside the circle. Each person took up a position about ten yards from where Autumn lay on the grass.

Keaton still didn't understand what all this was about, but he dutifully swallowed part of the leaf Winnie presented to him.

"It's to prevent the poison from attaching to us through the magic like it did Autumn and Chloe. An inoculation, if you will," Alastair explained. "We might still feel a bit sick afterward, but nothing life threatening."

"Hold your hands palm out on either side of your body," Spring instructed. "We are going to be a conduit for the magic."

Keaton did as he was told, facing his left palm toward Alastair's outstretched hand and his right palm toward Spring.

From across the distance, Preston nodded his approval.

"Are you really going to start this party without me?" a female voice questioned from behind Keaton.

He whipped his head around to see GiGi striding toward the group. Relief flooded through him. He'd seen her heal others twice before, and his confidence in her was strong. "Thank you, GiGi," he said feelingly.

"Of course, dear boy. She's my niece. Now, move over and make room."

She positioned herself between him and Alastair without sparing a glance for her brother. Apparently, she had no intention of acknowledging his existence.

"You need some of the plant, sister," Alastair stated with a nod in Winnie's direction. "We won't start until you can protect yourself."

Keaton observed her expression soften marginally.

Perhaps something good would come of this tragedy if saving Autumn was impossible. As soon as he thought it, he rejected the idea of her not returning to him. Isis was on their side.

Preston started to chant, calling on the Goddess and on his element. Bright-white light poured from his palms in an outward direction. Winnie and Nash joined in and channeled the light. Next were Alastair and Spring.

Keaton paid close attention to the language and the words. Soon enough it was time for him and GiGi to repeat the phrase and complete the circle.

When the ground rumbled beneath his feet, Keaton's nerves got the better of him. One-by-one, moss-covered ancient stones rose from their nesting place below the earth to encircle the group. Each stone stood roughly three to four feet in diameter and easily ten feet or more in height. If someone told him this was possible without him witnessing the process in action, he'd have called them a damned liar.

Although his voice trembled from his frayed nerves, he repeated the phrase as did the others until all the stones had settled in place.

"Take a few steps forward and join hands," GiGi instructed.

As one, the group shifted.

From his vantage point, Keaton could see the wide-eyed wonder on Derek's young face. He felt a kinship with the kid. The whole ceremony was awe inspiring.

"Alastair, what's next?" Preston asked.

Alastair nodded toward Autumn. "It's time for the Chintamani Stone to work its magic. Nash?"

"Everyone, call on your element. Use it to encapsulate the poison as it leaves her body. It's important you encase the mist completely to prevent it from reentering the host."

"This is like a movie where we have to get rid of the parasitic alien," Keaton muttered.

"You aren't wrong," Alastair laughed. "Put on your proverbial spacesuit, son, and get to work."

"What do we do with the poison once we remove it?" Keaton wanted to know.

"Direct it to the stone urn by her head. Preston, GiGi, and I will do the rest," Alastair instructed. "On the count of three. One... two... three."

Pulling from Autumn's past instruction, Keaton worked the magic in his cells, careful to push and not pulse the power. He lifted the water from the bowl by Autumn's left hip and held it steady until the black smoke-like substance emanated from her mouth and nose. All the elements attacked the mist at once, ripping it apart, wrapping around a section, and shoving it toward the urn opening.

Sweat beaded Keaton's brow and ran down the side of his temple. He struggled furiously to hold the poison. It fought like it had a life of its own. Just when he believed he had it contained, the damned thing would writhe and twist free.

"Control your power, boy!" Preston boomed.

The command added the extra edge Keaton needed—pure unadulterated fear of Autumn's father. Keaton had no intention of facing that man should he fail.

His was the last piece to go into the urn before the lid snapped into place. A golden rift opened in the center of the field. The air shimmered as it had in Autumn's bedroom. Except in place of the image stood his beloved's spirit. The ghost of her former self.

Beside her stood the most beautiful woman Keaton had ever laid eyes on.

Isis.

She had shimmering black hair piled high on her head, classical features—delicate, yet strong, and light amber eyes that glowed bright in the dark night. Her body was encased in a white off-the-shoulder dress belted by a gold rope chain. Her wide smile encompassed them all.

"Well done, my children. Very well done."

Isis focused her penetrating gaze on Keaton, and for a moment, he was lost but for the light shining from her entire being. Again, she smiled. "Take care of this gift I give you, my dear," she told him.

"I will," he promised.

With a regal nod, she snapped her fingers and called the urn to her. Then she retreated back into the opening. The sides of the rift sealed shut with a blinding gold light.

When he could peel open his eyelids, he noticed Autumn's spirit was gone.

Heart hammering, he broke the hold with Spring and Gigi to rush forward. He crashed to his knees at Autumn's side. "Babe?"

While her color was restored to normal, she didn't awaken.

"What's wrong? Why isn't she waking up?" he cried frantically.

GiGi laid a hand on his shoulder. "Patience, dear boy. She has to get used to the physical body again." Her words offered hope and calmed him.

"Maybe you should kiss Snow White," Nash said with a lopsided grin.

"Snow White?" Keaton asked in confusion.

"Snow White was poisoned by the wicked stepmother, had seven dwarfs, was laid out in a clearing... Not dissimilar to Autumn. Except she was poisoned by Lin, and we aren't dwarfs. The only thing she needs is the Prince to kiss her awake." Nash laughed and gave him a slight shove. "That's you in case you're too dense to understand."

Keaton wasn't fool enough to believe his kiss could wake her. But he leaned over and pressed his lips to Autumn's all the same. Into the soft kiss, he poured all the love in his heart. All the yearning from his soul. He hadn't realized he was crying until he pulled back and a single tear fell onto her pale cheek.

When her eyelashes fluttered and her breathing deepened, Keaton buried his face against her throat. "I love you, Autumn."

A cool hand cupped the nape of his neck, and the fingers stroked the hair there. In that second, he knew she'd returned to him.

"Our work here is done," Alastair quipped with a clap of his hands. "Who's in charge of hiding the clearing stones?"

CHAPTER 23

*A*utumn found her physical body much heavier since her stay in the Otherworld. While there, she only had to think about a destination to get from place to place, not unlike the magical teleporting, but it required no effort at all.

Two days had passed since Autumn woke in the glen, and there was a piece of her that missed the afterlife. Missed the beauty and thrill of her place beside Isis. Missed her mother with whom she'd gotten to reconnect and spend time. Missed just sitting beside a glorious lake and debating the meaning of life with those who'd left it far behind.

While she'd been unconscious mere days here, she thrived for weeks on end there. Heartaches and hurts had quickly dissolved into nothingness—as if they had never existed. The only thing remembered or felt had been love.

Over the last few days, Keaton had split his time between her and Chloe. And while Autumn tried to indicate he should take care of his daughter, he insisted he could do both. Today was one such day.

A light knock sounded on her bedroom door before it inched open. Keaton carried a tray into the room.

"Good morning, babe."

She stared at him dispassionately.

His smile dimmed.

"Still not speaking?"

She shrugged. It wasn't as if she'd lost her ability to talk. Or at least she didn't believe so. No, it was her *will* to talk that had taken a hike. Autumn had nothing to say that required vocalizing. Whatever she needed could be obtained with a simple jotted note if she was inclined.

Keaton set the tray across her lap. On it, he'd arranged a daisy in a vase and a giant cinnamon roll, dripping with icing.

"I thought maybe we could share."

Again, she shrugged, inched the tray toward him, then turned her face to the window.

"Are you mad at me? Is that why you are treating me this way?" he asked softly. "Because I was an ass to you the day Chloe fell ill?"

She faced him and sighed before she shook her head.

"Then why?"

His tortured gaze left her cold. No compassion, no desire to ease his plight, no feeling whatsoever warmed her. With a grimace, she shook her head. There was no way to explain.

"Do you want me to leave?" he finally choked out.

If she said yes, she suspected she would damage their relationship for good. But she also didn't want him around. Not yet. Not until she came back to herself—*if she ever did.*

In place of answering, she ripped off a small chunk of the roll and popped it in her mouth. She attempted a smile, but the food tasted like sawdust in her mouth. Without bothering to be ladylike, she spit the food into a napkin and frowned.

"Is something wrong with it?" he asked, puzzled.

She nodded and mock shuddered.

Keaton tore off a piece of the pastry and popped it into his mouth. He chewed and swallowed with no sign of disgust. "Tastes great to me."

Disquiet stirred in her breast. Either he was messing with her, or the food was fine.

She mimed a drink.

With a wide smile, he conjured a cup of coffee for her.

After a tentative sip, she held the cup to him to try.

"It's just the way you like it. Which is to say, it's too sweet for me," he laughed and tried to hand her the mug.

With an emphatic shake of her head, Autumn held up her hands.

"You have to eat or drink something, babe."

Hadn't she eaten since she'd been awake?

On her nightstand rested a pen and pad of paper. She picked them up and asked that exact question.

"No," he said after reading what she'd written. "You reject everything anyone brings you."

How long? she wrote.

"Since you've eaten? Two days. You take a bite and spit it out. You don't remember?"

Why couldn't she recall?

Get me Alastair, please.

Keaton took an inordinately long time reading the request. When he finally looked up from the notepad concern for her radiated from his eyes. "Is something wrong, Autumn? Tell me now."

I don't know. I feel nothing. I taste nothing. Want nothing, except...

He read her words and nodded thoughtfully. "Except?"

I want to go back.

"No!" He grabbed her hands and gave them a quick, hard shake. "Don't ever say that again. We'll figure this out," he stated more calmly. "Give me time. Please."

Meeting his probing gaze was too difficult, and she avoided looking at him. Instead, she wrote, *Alastair.*

"Okay."

She sighed her relief. Part of her knew Alastair held the key.

Once in the hallway, Keaton leaned back against the wall outside Autumn's room and gulped in large quantities of air.

I feel nothing. I taste nothing. Want nothing, except... I want to go back.

Her words freaked him right the fuck out. What was wrong with her? Why was she only a shell of her former self?

He supposed her lackluster response to life could be a direct result of her near death. But Chloe and Derek had returned to normal upon waking. Keaton couldn't understand what was different in Autumn's recovery.

Since Autumn seemed to think Alastair was key, Keaton intended to drag him here—kicking and screaming if he must.

Keaton hurried downstairs and grabbed the first Thorne he ran into. "Winnie, I need a contact number for Alastair."

Her alarmed gaze flew wide. "Why?"

"Autumn. She's... *off* since she's come back. You must've noticed."

She gnawed her lip in indecision. Finally, she said, "I'll get his number from Summer and call him." Before she finished speaking, Winnie had her smartphone out and had shot Summer a text. Within a minute, her phone pinged in return. She held up the device as he copied the number to his own.

"Thanks."

"Are you sure you want to summon him?"

"You make him sound like Lucifer," he chuckled, but his insides were a jumble of raw nerves. Alastair Thorne was one of two men who terrified the bejeezus out of him.

"Just be careful, Keaton. I suspect his help comes with a price."

He nodded and stepped outside to place the call.

Five minutes later, Alastair sat on the edge of Autumn's bed.

"Hello, niece."

"Uncle."

Keaton reeled in shock. "You spoke!" he said accusingly.

Her dispassionate gaze matched Alastair's as they stared at him.

"I'm just saying…" Keaton started. What the hell was he saying? He should shut up while he could. "I'll be over here," he muttered.

He caught the flash of amusement in Alastair's stare before the other man shifted his attention back to Autumn.

"Why am I here?"

"I'm cold inside. Everything is off. I thought you might know what is wrong with me."

A troubled expression crossed Alastair's countenance. Autumn's uncle cleared his throat. "I don't know how much you know of my past…" he began.

She cut him off with a wave of her hand. "All of it."

"I suspected as much. Isis does love to tell her tales," Alastair said dryly.

"Not Isis. My mom."

The air in the room crackled with tension. "You spoke to Aurora?" The husky quality to Alastair's voice left little doubt how much the man loved Autumn's mother. "She's okay?"

"She is." Autumn met his gaze straight on. "She said you were in the Otherworld for a long while before returning. Back when Lin held you captive."

Alastair's features froze in icy rage.

Keaton's gut tightened in response, but he stepped forward anyway. He'd protect Autumn until his last breath if he had to.

"Calm down, boy. I'm not going to hurt her," Alastair snapped without sparing him a glance. The older man rose to his feet in one elegant gesture. He moved to the window and stared at the vista on the other side of the glass pane.

Keaton's gaze connected with Autumn's. She didn't look nearly as ruffled as he felt. Apparently, she wasn't concerned with pissing off the almighty warlock.

"When the Désorcelers captured me, they took me to the monastery where you were held. That same quaint little dungeon in fact. I was left to rot with others, who soon became those corpses you had the misfortune to encounter." Alastair spun around and pinned them with an emotionless stare. "Some of those skeletons had been my brothers-in-arms. One-by-one, we were taken out, tortured, and returned to the cell to sit in our own blood and filth."

He addressed Keaton. "I sent you into the cell to retrieve my niece because I couldn't set foot in there. Not again."

"How did you escape?" Keaton asked quietly.

"I died."

Whatever answer Keaton had been expecting, that wasn't it. He shook his head in confusion. "I don't understand."

"I died and went to the Otherworld. Isis kept my body in stasis until I could return. Her gift to me—her descendent." Alastair gestured with a scarred hand to Autumn. "And I suspect her gift to Autumn as well. She loves her family fiercely and will bend the cosmic rules to save us if she can."

With the standard Thorne shrug of his shoulders, Alastair walked to stand beside Autumn's bed. He held out his hand to her. She rose with his assistance and faced him.

"How long did it take for the cold to go away, Uncle?"

"I doubt it ever does. A piece of it will always stay with you. But I will do for you what another did for me." So saying, he placed one palm flat over her heart and the other horizontally across her forehead. "Breathe and let the magic flow through you. Pull it deep into your cells and let it warm you again."

A red glow infused Autumn's eyes, brightening her irises to amber from muddy brown. Her back arched, and her mouth dropped open in a silent scream.

"You're hurting her!" Keaton yelled as he surged forward.

"Stay back, boy!" Alastair barked. "*Never* make the mistake of interrupting a spell."

"But—"

"Shut the fuck up!"

Keaton bristled with the need to challenge Alastair, but by the time he got his balls in hand to do just that, Alastair had stepped away from Autumn.

"How do you feel?" he asked her.

She turned luminous eyes on her uncle. "Almost normal."

"Each passing day you will feel more yourself."

"Thank you, Uncle."

"My pleasure, child." He gestured to Keaton with a side nod. "Teach this one manners before he gets someone hurt or killed."

In a blink, Alastair was gone.

Keaton rushed to haul her close. "He didn't hurt you? You looked like you were in agony," he said gruffly.

"He was helping me. Yes, it hurt, but sometimes magic does."

"What was that? What did he do?"

She shook her head in a helpless manner. "I guess the best way to describe it would be to say he restored the balance to my cells. They'd been in a death-like state too long, I think. It made returning impossible without his help."

"How do you know all this?"

"As he infused his power into my body, the knowledge came with it. I don't know how it's done to be honest." She smiled and placed her palm along his clenched jaw. "I'll take that cinnamon roll now."

Keaton closed his eyes in relief. "Welcome back, babe."

"You know what I really want?" she asked a short while later.

"What's that?"

"To see my daughter." She laughed in the face of his confusion. "Chloe was ours first. The baby I lost. Apparently, she was determined to be born regardless."

He had no words. Chloe had mentioned Autumn was her mother when she woke up a few days ago. He had assumed it was a child's flight of fancy.

"You look shell-shocked," she said. "Isis said it was so. Her words were something along the lines of Chloe and me being linked for many incarnations."

"Reincarnation is real?" Raised in a small town, with small town beliefs, it wasn't easy to grasp things on a larger scale. While he'd always considered himself open-minded—with the exception of his reaction to Autumn's confession years ago—it took him longer to wrap his head around the things revealed to him through the magical community.

"It is," she assured him. "Come on, let's finish here, and I can tell you about all the times you, me, and Chloe were a family."

"Are you truly back?" he asked, afraid of the answer.

"Mostly. Like Alastair said, there is a part that feels off. Not in a terrible way. Just distanced from the rest of me."

"What the hell does that mean?"

"I don't know, Keaton. But let's put it behind us for a little while. I want to taste food again. To savor the sweetness of the air. Spend time with you and Chloe. Can we do that without the twenty questions?"

He nodded and took the hand she offered, knowing he'd go anywhere she cared to lead him.

CHAPTER 24

*D*uring their meal that afternoon, Autumn half-listened to Chloe chatter about whatever it was little girls liked to discuss without end. Periodically, Keaton would shoot a worried glance her way. Autumn would smile her reassurance.

She understood his concern. From the moment Keaton heard Alastair say that not all of the coldness goes away, he'd been worried. But the hovering-helicopter act was getting on her last nerve.

Only time would cure what ailed her. But neither of them would make it long enough to find out if he didn't stop checking on her every five minutes. Granted, she'd only been revived a few days ago, but physically, she felt fine.

Autumn needed a diversion and had just the thing. "I think it's time we summon your familiars."

Chloe's head whipped around, and the joyful light in her honey eyes made Autumn smile.

"I'm assuming you'd like that?"

Keaton frowned. "Do you have one? I've never seen you with an animal."

Of course, he hadn't. She'd never called one to her. In the past, she'd borrowed her mother's temperamental old cat for spells.

After Autumn's mother had left, loving or depending on another living being wasn't something she'd been ready for. Or at least she hadn't been until she'd hooked up with Keaton.

In the time they were dating, she hadn't spared a thought to finding a familiar. Afterward, their breakup and the loss of the baby caused her to shut down her heart. A familiar needed a strong emotional connection to be effective.

"The timing was never right for me. But it is now. I say let's have a ceremony. What do you think?" She infused fake cheer into her question.

His keen gaze missed nothing, but he nodded anyway. "Sure. I say we do this thing. Uh, how *do* we do this thing?"

Chloe giggled. "Daddy, you're so silly. That's what Mama is going to show us."

Autumn sucked in her breath and stared. She hadn't given much thought to moving forward other than that she knew she wanted to spend time with Chloe whenever possible. But being called "Mama" brought their relationship to a whole new level.

Chloe's happiness faded to worry. "Is it okay if I call you Mama?"

Locked in place, Autumn could only stare.

"Babe?" An edge of strong emotion lurked in the single word. Yet, Autumn remained unable to acknowledge him.

Tears flooded the young girl's eyes, but still Autumn couldn't speak.

"I thought since Isis…" Chloe mumbled the beginning of her explanation then trailed off and cast her eyes downward.

Autumn was out of her seat and around the table in an instant. She hauled the little girl into her embrace and buried her nose in Chloe's strawberry scented hair.

"It's more than okay, kid," Autumn whispered fiercely. "So much more than okay."

Over Chloe's dark head, Autumn sought Keaton's approval. His wide grin eased her insecurities. She cleared her throat. "How about we find our familiars now?"

"Why don't you already have one, Mama?"

"I wasn't ready," she answered honestly. "I needed to be receptive and open for the Goddess to grant me that type of gift." Autumn hugged Chloe again and said, "But I think you helped me with that."

Chloe's sunny smile warmed another vital area of Autumn's soul.

Holding back her own smile became impossible. "Let's do this thing! Race you to the clearing!"

Mischief danced across Chloe's face, and Autumn grabbed Keaton's hand without warning.

His confusion was short-lived as she teleported them both to the glen. Chloe was a mere second behind.

"Nice!" Autumn laughed. "Have you been practicing these last couple days?"

"Only to the barn and back. Uncle Knox has been helping me," Chloe admitted.

"How did I not know this?" Keaton demanded in mock outrage. "And when do I get to try?"

Autumn and Chloe shared a laughing glance.

"Okay, first things first. I need to cloak the area," Autumn declared. "We can't have people stumbling upon our ritual."

"What can I do?" Chloe asked.

"Never try this until I say you're ready," Autumn infused sternness into her words. "I mean it, Chloe. I promise to teach you when the time is right, but it's advanced magic. Do you understand?"

After she received the nod of agreement, Autumn lifted her hands skyward and voiced the incantation. A slight pulse of the atmosphere around them was the only indication the spell had taken effect.

"Now we cast the circle. Chloe, do you remember how this is done?"

"Am I allowed to do it?"

"I'd be honored to have you start the ceremony. Keep in mind, this one may take time. We need to call our animal to us and wait until it appears. If it hasn't appeared within the hour, we close the circle and try again another day." While she spoke, Autumn conjured ingredients they needed along with the athame and blanket.

She handed Chloe the candles to light and proudly watched as the child cast the perfect circle. Once the girl had finished, Autumn clasped hands with her and Keaton.

"Repeat after me…

"By the Goddess's divine will
Fur, feather, fin, or scale
I call unto thee.
Creature of the earth,
Please, come assist me.
Honor, light, and love
I shall provide for thee.
As it will, so mote it be."

They repeated the chant in all four directions: north, east, south, and west. Once the call went out, they sat to wait.

Chloe's familiar was the first to arrive. From the air, a hawk swooped down and landed on the ground before her. "What do I do?" she asked in a loud whisper.

Autumn bit her lip to hide her amusement. "Now, you ask the hawk its name, and solemnly request he assist you in your future magical endeavors."

The child frowned as if trying to memorize the exact wording Autumn put forth.

"You don't have to be quite that specific, sweetie. Speak to your new friend how you would speak to anyone else. But remember, he's here because he wants to be. You don't command him; you *request*."

After Chloe established a rapport with the bird, Keaton's familiar appeared in the shape of an otter.

"I'm not like you and Chloe, I can't hear animals respond," he said.

"Because you aren't listening, Keaton," Autumn admonished. "Quiet your mind and let her show you the pictures in hers."

It took a good twenty minutes, but Keaton finally understood the concept of sharing thoughts with his new spirit animal. Before long, the otter was curled up in Keaton's lap and staring up at Keaton as if he created the stars and moon.

"Another female conquest," Autumn muttered in disgust. "Good luck getting that one to do anything but stare at your beautiful face."

His wicked grin tickled her lady spot.

She rolled her eyes and checked her watch. Only another ten minutes, and she'd have to give up on finding a familiar of her own this time around.

"What do you think yours is going to be, Mama?" Chloe asked the question utmost in Autumn's mind.

"I have no idea. But if we continue the element theme, probably Smoky the Bear," she laughed.

They didn't have much longer to wait. A shuffling sounded to the right and Autumn turned her head to greet the newcomer. A massive wolf with fur the most incredible shades of red she'd ever seen hesitated at the edge of the tree line. The beast cocked his head and met Autumn's gaze across the distance.

She couldn't contain her smile. "I'm fortunate in the Goddess's choice."

The wolf loped to where she knelt then rubbed his large jaw along hers.

"What is he doing?" Keaton asked. Worry made his tone sharper than necessary.

"He's marking me. We're bonding."

"I didn't know wolves lived in this area, and certainly not ones that large. Chloe, I think you need to make sure you aren't wandering these woods alone from here on out."

His nervous energy affected the other animals in the circle. The hawk took flight, and the otter tried to burrow deeper in his lap, although Autumn had her doubts about whether the thing was actually hiding or not.

Her new familiar growled low in its throat.

"Easy, Red. Keaton's no threat to you, just as you're no threat to him. We are all a pack," Autumn soothed with a meaningful glance in Keaton's direction. "The magical community has nothing to fear from nature's creatures. We co-exist in all things."

"But—"

She cut off Keaton's objections. "You would know that if you were raised properly," she said sharply. "Don't let your fear and ignorance get in the way. Chloe needs to approach learning with an open mind."

KEATON DIDN'T CARE FOR AUTUMN'S TONE, BUT HE UNDERSTOOD the warning behind her words. His built-in beliefs could alter how Chloe perceived things. Still, *a wolf*! And a fucking massive beast at that! He'd be lying if he said the predator didn't make him nervous as hell.

"Pet him. Show him we are a pack," Autumn encouraged him and Chloe.

Chloe surged forward, eager in her excitement.

It took every ounce of willpower not to jerk her into the safety of his arms.

"He's soft and warm," Chloe laughed. "I love him."

The wolf sat on his haunches and allowed Chloe to hug his neck. With his tongue lolled out the side of his mouth, the canine resembled nothing more than an oversized dog.

Keaton centered himself and dispelled his concerns before he shifted forward to run a hand down the length of Red's back. "He's beautiful," he breathed in awe.

Red rewarded him with a swipe of his tongue along Keaton's cheek. The gesture cemented their tentative friendship.

"Okay. Now it's time for us to close the circle and return home. Keaton, would you like to do the honors?"

He performed the closing as he'd been taught weeks before. A sense of peace came with the knowledge that he was becoming more comfortable in his new life. His only remaining issue was Lin—and the ever-present knowledge the bastard would strike again. Between now and that time, Keaton would prepare. He would learn all he could and find a way to neutralize the threat to Autumn, Chloe, and the rest of their extended family. Perhaps Alastair and Preston had some ideas toward that end goal.

As Keaton and Autumn walked hand-in-hand behind his skipping, chattering daughter, the realization came to him that, in this moment, he had all he'd ever wanted. He jerked to a stop and swung Autumn around to face him.

"Marry me."

"Pardon?"

"Marry me," he said again. "Let's be a family. You, me, Chloe."

When she stared at him without responding, trepidation snuck in. What did she see when she looked at him now? Could she ever see beyond the mistakes he'd made in the past? Inasmuch as she'd said she'd put his transgression behind her, had she really?

"I need time, Keaton."

Her words sounded like a death knell for their relationship.

"That's a no," he stated heavily.

"No, it's not a no. It's an 'I need time'," she replied with a squeeze of his hand. "The last time we talked marriage was nearly ten years ago. It didn't end well. At that point, we'd been dating for ten months." She dropped his hand and began pacing. "How can I explain this in a way that makes you see this isn't a rejection?" She paused and faced him. "You've only been back in my life less than a month. You're acting like we can pick up where we left off. As if we haven't changed or grown into different people."

"We love each other, Autumn. That's never going to change regardless of the passing of time," he argued. "Isn't that the point?"

"No. Two people can love one another and still not be right for each other."

"Wow! What was all of this? Your attempt at revenge?" He ran shaking hands through his hair. "Draw me back in and then crush my heart?"

Her sad, dark eyes tore at his insides. Only twenty minutes earlier they'd been a light amber, exuding happiness. "Your accusation proves you don't know me. That you've never known me," she told him softly.

"Christ, babe. I'm sorry. I'm being an ass because I'm hurt," he said gruffly. "I don't believe you slept with me for revenge. Not when I was the one pushing for a relationship." He stared off into the distance and registered the darkening sky. The coming storm matched his mood. Her hand on his arm startled him.

"I don't want to fight. I only wanted more time for us to get to know each other again."

"I know." He studied the fine features of her face, taking in the thinness from the few days she'd been in stasis. "When you were lost to me these last few days, I nearly went out of my mind. It killed me that the last words I said to you were in anger." Keaton tucked a lock of her wild hair behind the delicate shell of her ear. Loathe to stop touching her, he traced the length of her jaw and rubbed a thumb softly along her full, lower lip. "I don't want to ever feel that way again. When you walk away this time, know that I love you. I will always love you. And no matter when, or if, you ever decide to return to me, I'll be waiting."

Tears pooled in her eyes, and he felt the matching sting in his own.

"I *do* love you, Keaton."

Without a word he opened his arms to her, and she walked into his embrace. Keaton rested his forehead against hers. "When I hold you like this, I have hope. It makes me never want to let you go."

Autumn drew back and met his gaze purposefully. "Let's make a pact," she suggested. "In four months' time, if we are both of the same mind, we'll readdress your proposal."

He frowned. "Both of the same mind? My mind is set and will never change."

She smiled. "Four months."

"Four months," he agreed with a gentle kiss.

CHAPTER 25

"*P*ow wow at Thorne Manor in ten."

Keaton glanced up from the Carlyle family grimoire he'd been studying. "This about Alastair's next scavenger hunt item, C.C.?"

"Something like that. I think there might be talk of Lin's location."

"He's been found?" Keaton asked sharply. He prayed it was true. He had a score to settle.

"Knox has information on someone fitting Lin's description."

"I'll be right there."

"Mom's agreed to keep an eye on Chloe," Coop informed him.

"Perfect. Thanks."

Five minutes later, Keaton teleported to Autumn's home in Maine.

He'd caught her wrapped in a towel and grinned his delight. "Nice!"

"Perfect timing." She laughed and eased back the sides of the towel to give him a glimpse of the goods. "I was feeling a bit lonely."

"Ah, babe. As much as I want to jump all over that, Summer's called a family meeting."

Autumn pouted, dropped her towel, and cupped her breasts. "I guess I'll have to take matters into my own hands."

"Fuck the family meeting," he rasped as he dove for her.

Her happy laughter echoed through the hall as she ran for the bedroom. He beat her there by ten seconds.

"You're getting good at teleporting," she stated proudly.

He lifted her into his arms, laid her softly on the bed, and followed her down. "I had a great teacher."

"Mmhmm. You're just flattering me because you want to get laid."

"Is it working?"

"Absolutely!"

"Score!"

"You do realize if we do this, we are going to be seriously late?" she warned. The twinkle in her eye told him, she knew very well he didn't care about showing up a few minutes late to the meeting.

"I don't know about you, but I can get off in under three minutes. Especially, with you steering this boat."

"I need a little more handling."

"I've got you covered," he murmured against her lips as he cupped her gorgeous, full D's.

"You certainly do." Autumn guided his head to her erect nipple.

Fifteen minutes later, they arrived at Thorne Manor, out of breath and flushed. There could be no doubt in anyone's mind what had delayed them. Yet, Keaton didn't care if the whole world knew. The love he felt for his woman couldn't be contained.

He settled into an armchair and drew her down onto his lap. When Autumn wiggled her bottom, he gave a low warning growl for her ears alone. The little troublemaker did it on purpose.

"If you two are ready to actually join us, can we discuss the issue at hand?" Alastair's tone suggested he wasn't truly asking.

"C.C. told me Knox might have a location for Lin," Keaton said.

Autumn's head twisted to stare at him in surprise. "Why didn't you lead with that when you showed up at my house?"

A lifted brow and a smirk was all he offered by way of an answer.

"Point taken."

It was all he could do not to snort. A small part of him would always be twelve when it came to innuendoes and Autumn.

Coop, on the other hand, showed no such restraint and laughed. It earned him an elbow in the ribs from his girlfriend. Although, in truth, Summer looked as amused as Coop.

"Lin isn't the issue," Alastair said. "He'll get his in due course. However, the Uterine amulet is more important and next on the list to be recovered."

Autumn shifted forward. "Do we have an idea what we are looking for, and where?"

"The particular amulet we're seeking was carved from Jasper. Nearly black in color." Alastair passed around sketches of the object. "As to the where, the starting point is Egypt." He handed out a word document. "All that is known is in those three paragraphs. I'm counting on the ten of you to figure this out."

"Ten?" Winnie asked, glancing around at their group. "Uncle, there are only nine of us."

Alastair's smile struck Keaton as odd. It was as if Winnie had stepped into a verbal trap.

"There will be ten as soon as you bring Zane Carlyle into the fold," Alastair stated.

Winnie's adverse reaction made Keaton wonder if it was Alastair's attitude or the thought of Zane joining their group that had her up in arms.

"I don't believe Zane has anything to contribute." Winnie lifted her chin haughtily.

A study of the room's occupants showed them all to be as surprised as Keaton. Interesting. Apparently, Winnie and Zane had history no one knew anything about.

"And yet he does," Alastair countered smoothly. "He has a vast knowledge of all things Egyptian. He minored in archaeology."

"Don't tell me, the amulet needs to be excavated, and only Zane has the skills?" Winnie grimaced when Alastair's smile widened. "Fine. We'll invite Zane into our ever-expanding group."

"I don't need to warn you to keep this among yourselves, do I?" he asked with an arrogant lift to his dark-blond brow. "If the Witches' Council gets wind of this, they'll send Nash or Preston after the amulet. We need it to revive Aurora."

"We know how to utilize stealth and cunning when needed," Summer assured him.

"Good. On that note, I will leave you all to plan your next adventure." He focused on Winnie. "Might I suggest you be the one to retrieve it?"

"Why me?" she demanded.

"Your ability to manipulate air will come in handy."

Without another word or an explanation as to why Winnie's element would come into play, Alastair disappeared with a simple snap of his fingers.

"Does anyone else have the feeling our Uncle Alastair just set me up?" Winnie asked sourly.

"No doubt about it," Summer laughed. "He totally did. The question is why?"

"If it's a problem, Winnie, I can go in your place," Autumn offered.

"No. You've been through enough and need to continue helping Keaton and Coop master their magic." Winnie crinkled her nose. "I can deal. But does anyone know when Zane plans to return?"

"He's actually in the process of moving his practice to Leiper's Fork," Knox informed them. "He bought out Peterson's firm in town."

"Other than to consult on Alastair's amulet, what can he truly do?" Keaton asked. "When Mom and Dad unbound our powers, he didn't regain his."

Winnie's head whipped in his direction so fast, Keaton suspected she suffered whiplash. "He is supposed to have abilities too?" Her voice rose high enough to shatter glass.

"That's what Dad said," he confirmed.

"I have to go." Her chalky expression prefaced her disappearing act.

"I wonder what that was all about?" he asked aloud.

"Anyone else get the feeling Winnie and Zane had a run in at some point?" Autumn asked on a laugh.

Summer nodded and rose from her position next to Coop. "Absolutely. That dirty holdout! I intend to get to the bottom of this one."

"Let her be, Nosy Nellie." Coop stood and wrapped his arms around her. "You and I have other important things to do."

The wicked grin on his brother's face told Keaton exactly what those "important things" were. Spring must've understood the significance too because she screwed up her face and muttered "Eww" under her breath.

"That's my cue to leave," Spring added. "I have a date I need to prepare for."

"*A date?*"

All heads turned in Knox's direction when he snapped the question—all but Spring's. She continued to ignore Knox's existence as she had the entire meeting.

In an aside to Autumn, Keaton murmured, "Do you get the feeling this is like a bizarre play unfolding?"

"All we need is popcorn to enjoy the show," she returned as quietly.

Spring strutted from the room with Knox storming behind like an over-protective guardian.

"I really wish they'd had it out here. I wanted to find out what that was all about," Holly complained. "I miss everything."

"Why worry about their lover's spat when you and I can while away the hours in more pleasant pursuits, my little prickly pear?" Quentin attempted to bury his face in Holly's neck and was met with a palm to his face.

"Get a life, loser," she snapped before teleporting away.

Quentin sighed heavily, and for once, Keaton sympathized with the man. He still didn't like the guy, but at least he could understand the frustration of chasing a female who pretended to hate you.

Their eyes connected across the distance of the living room, and Quentin shot him a self-deprecating half smile. Five seconds later, he followed Holly's lead and disappeared.

"I almost feel bad for him," Keaton said.

"I know what you mean. She's pretty harsh when it comes to Quentin."

"And yet she allows him to follow her around. What's up with that?"

"I believe it's because he was hired by Alastair to protect her," Autumn said with a shrug. "It doesn't matter. They'll either work out their differences, or they won't."

"Like us?" he asked softly.

"I think we got lucky," she returned with a kiss to his lips.

"I know I did," he replied softly. "I love you, Autumn Thorne."

"I love you, Keaton Carlyle."

AUTUMN TOUCHED HER NOSE TO KEATON'S IN A LIGHT ESKIMO KISS. "Let's leave Summer and Coop alone and go find Chloe. I think it's time for a picnic in the clearing."

"I'd think you'd want to avoid that place." Keaton helped her to her feet and stood beside her.

"I learned a new appreciation for it on the other side." At Keaton's frown, she explained, "There is old magic based there. Our minutes of hurt are nothing in the timeline of its history."

"I know what you mean. It was always one of my favorite places to be prior to our breakup. Even afterward, I found myself wandering there to reflect on life now and again."

"I didn't know that."

Pink dusted his cheekbones. "It made me feel closer to you somehow."

"I thought you hated me."

"Never. Even when I was furious with you, babe, I never hated you. You were my reason for breathing."

"Oh, Keaton."

"Shhh, let's not go there again. We have our whole lives to look forward to."

He was right—Autumn knew that—yet, some days the past snuck up and tried to grab her in its stranglehold. On those days, she had to work to remember she now held the upper hand. She had Isis in her corner and, hopefully, no more misunderstandings on the horizon.

"I don't need four months," she blurted.

"What?"

"I don't need four months. If you'll still have me, I'll marry you."

Shocked, Keaton didn't respond.

She smiled into the face of his disbelief.

"You mean it?" he croaked.

"With all my heart."

With a happy cry, he wrapped her in his warm embrace. "How soon?"

"I don't need anything elaborate. A quick ceremony in the clearing works for me." She laughed between the kisses he rained on her. "But I have one condition."

He drew back a little warily. "What's that?"

"Chloe has to agree this is what she wants for us as a family."

"I don't think that is going to be a problem. She's nagged me from day one, telling me she wants you for her mom."

"Shall we go ask her?" she suggested.

"Hold on."

Keaton teleported them to the Carlyle estate with ease.

"Nice job!"

He grinned and bussed her lips. "Thanks."

Together they sought out Chloe where she was bent over her schoolwork.

Her response was better than they could've imagined.

"Do you want to wait until we wake Aurora?" Keaton asked her later that night as they lay in bed.

Autumn turned the idea over in her mind before rejecting it. "No. She may never wake. I don't want to waste any more time. I think she would understand."

"Am I being too much of an asshole if I leave the planning up to you?"

She laughed and rolled on her stomach to look down on him. "You can do as much or as little as you want. It will mainly be about the people surrounding and supporting us. Everything else is just decoration."

"But what about dresses, the cake, and that sort of thing?"

"The dress is a simple snap of my fingers. As for the cake, I'll let Winnie know your favorite flavor, and she can create one of her masterpieces." She traced his pec with her index finger. "I swear she should've opened a bakery instead of an online lotion shop. That woman can cook!"

"I'm not going to lie; if you hadn't accepted my proposal, I was going to ask her next. Those cinnamon rolls are incredible."

She laughed again and rested her head over his heart. "I can see the attraction."

Keaton held out his hand and closed his eyes. Within seconds, a ring rested in his palm.

Her eyes widened at the beauty of the design. A square emerald-cut amber jewel was outlined with brilliant diamonds. The precious stone captured the inner radiance in such a way as to make it appear as if a flame danced within its center.

"Ohmygod, Keaton! It's gorgeous!"

"It matches your eyes." He lifted her left hand and slid the ring in place. "Perfect—like you."

Moisture flooded her eyes and, one-by-one, her tears escaped to trek down her cheeks. "I don't know what to say."

"Just tell me you love me, and it will be more than enough."

"I love you."

"You are my world, Autumn Thorne. Never forget that."

EPILOGUE

ONE WEEK LATER

*T*oday was the day.

Stomach a ball of excitement, Autumn Thorne cut through the dense woods, making her way to the clearing where Keaton would be waiting.

All four of her sisters trailed behind, with Chloe alongside her, their hands clasped together. The girl happily prattled on about everything under the sun. When they reached the glen, Keaton stood waiting within the circle of the ancient stones. He dazzled in his black tuxedo.

Nerves almost got the better of Autumn, and in a moment of blind panic, she considered fleeing. The nervous expression on Keaton's face along with the worried look in his Caribbean-blue gaze made the difference. She noted the color of his eyes, and it stopped her from a foolish knee-jerk reaction due to her own apprehension. Since they'd put the past behind them, his irises had gradually shifted back to the color they had been when they were wildly in love as young adults.

And as Autumn paused to watch him, Keaton adjusted his cufflinks twice and straightened his bowtie at least three times. A good portion of her own anxiety dissipated. The scars of the past marked them both. But now was the time to let it all go. To step up and repeat the vows that would bind them for life.

"Mama?" The one word held all Chloe's questions.

Autumn glanced down into the child's fearful face and smiled. "Are we ready to do this thing, kid?"

Happiness bloomed on the young girl's face, and she took her position with the flower basket. Autumn watched Chloe with pride and all the love she held for the child.

Her hand came to rest on her lower abdomen. Soon enough there would be another child to love. She still couldn't believe the gift the Goddess had given her during her stasis. Where once she couldn't have children, now she could once more.

"Are you ready?" The deep voice startled her from her musings.

Autumn turned her attention to her father. "I believe I am."

"Ten years ago, I would've said he wasn't worthy of you. And perhaps he still isn't, but then no one's good enough for my beloved daughter," Preston said gruffly. "You tell him he'd better treat you right or he has me to answer to."

"I will, Dad."

Preston extended his arm, and Autumn took it without reservation. Together they waited for Chloe to deposit the rest of her yellow daisy petals on the path.

Across the distance, Autumn met Keaton's warm, loving gaze and smiled with all the joy in her heart. His return grin lit up the clearing.

As she made her way down the aisle, her cream-colored lace train trailed behind, stirring the lush, fragrant grass. The few guests —mostly family and Derek—rose as she passed.

Phinneas Flynn, head of the Witches' Council and the person who would perform their commitment ceremony, stepped forward as Autumn approached. In his hands, he held a metal bowl and a long white cloth shot through with silver threads—the hand-fasting material handed down through her family line from Isis.

"Are you ready, Autumn?"

"I am."

He faced Keaton.

"Are you ready, Keaton?"

"I am," Keaton confirmed.

"Let's proceed."

As Phinneas droned on about the sanctity of marriage, of the Goddess, and of magic, Keaton clasped her hand and lifted it to his lips. The gesture was so sweet, so perfect in the moment, it stole her breath away.

Autumn tightened her fingers in the hopes she could relay what she felt.

"Who has the rings?" Phinneas asked.

"I've got that taken care of," Autumn said with a side glance in Keaton's direction. She faced the crowd. "Summer."

Her sister released her pet chimpanzee, Morty, to approach with a small white pillow in his hands.

Keaton paled but remained still as Autumn bent to retrieve the pillow with the rings.

"Thank you, Sir Mortimer. Can you show Keaton there's no hard feelings?"

The small ape bent at the waist, then curled his lip back in a grin before ambling back to Summer.

"Not funny, babe," Keaton said in an aside. "That chimp is an asshole. He tried to use my head for batting practice."

"Oh, it's a little funny," she returned with a smirk. "What did you call him? The Babe Ruth of apes?"

"The Babe Ruth of Chimps, and that was C.C. I was—*wait!* How did you even know about that conversation? If I recall correctly, you were making good your escape after firebombing my truck."

"Old Man Harkins was kind enough to let me review his tapes," she said with a grin.

Keaton's eyes narrowed. "We reviewed those tapes, and they didn't have anything of interest."

"They certainly did. But that's what witchcraft is for."

"How many other things have you gotten away with over the years?"

"I think, as the town Mayor, you shouldn't ask a loaded question like that," she said as she handed him a ring.

"I think, as the town Mayor, I'm lucky you're now on my side," he retorted without heat, dropping a quick kiss on her lips. "Will you quit stalling and marry me?"

She winked and faced Phinneas, who watched them with wry amusement.

They exchanged rings and joined hands. Around their wrists, Phinneas wove the sacred hand-fasting cloth as a symbol of unity. From the metal bowl, he anointed them with the oil it contained.

"Lavender for devotion to one another. Myrtle for wedded bliss. Thyme for strength in the face of all challenges the Goddess puts in your path. And lastly, yarrow for everlasting love," he said. "May you bask in the happiness the Goddess will afford you. Blessed be."

The entire party repeated the words "blessed be."

"You may kiss your bride, Keaton."

Keaton grinned, and Autumn felt it down to her very toes. As he leaned in, she said, "I love you, Keaton Carlyle. I always have, and I always will."

The kiss was one of beauty. It held all the emotions of the past, and all the promise of the future.

"I love you, too, Autumn Carlyle. For now. For always."

———

ALASTAIR CLASPED HIS HAND ON HIS BROTHER'S SHOULDER. "TWO down. Three to go."

Preston shot him a sharp glance. "Are you matchmaking, brother?"

"I wouldn't call it matchmaking per se, but if I can help push Aurora's children in the direction of their soulmates..." Alastair shrugged and left the insinuation open to interpretation.

"I never thought I'd see the day when you went soft," GiGi said from behind the two men.

"Never soft, dear sister. Perhaps a bit sentimental, but never soft."

"Who's next on your list?" Preston asked.

"Winnie and Zane."

GiGi choked.

Both men turned inquiring gazes upon her.

Alastair was the first to respond. "Something we should know, sister?"

"That one might be a bit difficult," she confessed, color creeping up her neck.

"What did you do?" Preston asked.

"*I* didn't do anything," she said with a shrug. "*Winnie* on the other hand…"

Alastair heaved a long-suffering sigh. "Why am I always forced to clean up this family's mess?"

Preston chuckled. "You always did love a challenge, brother. It seems you found it in the Thorne children."

With a distasteful grimace, Alastair disappeared.

"What *did* happen with Winnie and Zane?" Preston asked his sister.

"She might've cast a tiny spell that may or may not have had a side effect."

"Let me guess; you helped her," he said dryly.

"She was determined to do it anyway," GiGi defended.

"Well, if anyone is up for the task, it's our dear brother. But I definitely intend to watch this one unfold."

FROM THE AUTHOR...

Thank you for taking the time to read *AUTUMN MAGIC*. If you love what you've read, please leave a brief review. To find out about what's happening next in the world of The Thorne Witches, be sure to subscribe my newsletter.

www.tmcromer.com/newsletter

Books in The Thorne Witches Series:

SUMMER MAGIC
AUTUMN MAGIC
WINTER MAGIC
SPRING MAGIC

Never fear. Each of the characters you've come to love—Holly, Nash, Alastair, and GiGi—will have a story of their own in the coming months.

You can find my online media sites here:

Website: http://www.tmcromer.com
Facebook: http://www.facebook.com/tmcromer
TM Cromer's Reader Group:
http://www.facebook.com/groups/tmcromerfanpage
Twitter: http://www.twitter.com/tmcromer
Instagram: http://www.instagram.com/tmcromer

How to stay up-to-date on releases, news and other events...

✓ *Join my mailing list. My newsletter is filled with news on current releases, potential sales, new-to-you author introductions, and contests each month. But if it gets to be too much, you can unsub-scribe at any time. Your information will always be kept private. No spam here!*
www. tmcromer.com/newsletter

✓ *Sign up for text alerts. This is a great way to get a quick, no-nonsense message for when my books are released or go on sale. These texts are no more frequently than every few months. Text TMCBOOKS to 24587.*

✓ *Follow me on BookBub. If you are into the quick notification method, this one is perfect. They notify you when a new book is released. No long email to read, just a simple "Hey, T.M.'s book is out today!" www.bookbub.com/authors/t-m-cromer*

✓ *Follow me on retailer sites. If you buy most of your books in digital format, this is a perfect way to stay current on my new releases. Again, like BookBub, it is a simple release-day notification.*

✓ *Join my Facebook Reader Group. While the standard pages and profiles on Facebook are not always the most reliable, I have created a group for fans who like to interact. This group entitles readers to "reader group only" contests, as well as an exclusive first look at covers, excerpts and more. The Reader Group is the most fun way to follow yet! I hope to see you there!*
www.facebook.com/groups/tmcromerfanpage

AFTERWORD

According to Buddhist and Hindu legend, Chintamani Stone is a wish-fulfilling jewel that fell from the sky. This may be an indication that the stone was a piece of a meteorite. And while the Chintamani Stone was rumored to have actually existed, the object did indeed disappear around the 1920's.

Were Nicholas and Helena Roerich in possession of the stone? Possibly. It ties into the time the Roerich family spent in the Himalayas.

But the bottom line? I took a bit of creative license with the stone's power and with Helena's journal—*as writers are wont to do*—as I will also do with the artifacts listed in the coming stories for the Thorne sisters. I mean, that's the great part about being an author, isn't it?

If you care to learn more about Nicholas and Helena, you can find a link for the museum dedicated to the couple here: www.roerich.org.

Printed in Great Britain
by Amazon